ABOUT THIS BOOK

The fourth annual Havenwood Falls Short Story Anthology takes you back to your favorite small town in the mountains for the holidays.

It's been a challenging couple of years, but you can escape from it all by transporting to your favorite fictional town for the holidays. Ten brand new stories feature some of your favorite supernatural characters as they try to find a sense of peace among the holiday madness and family chaos, always with a dash—or more—of romantic tension.

Teeny Weeny Tahini discovers a curse on the town's trees; Micah Westbrook disappears while Sedona and Holly are snowed in at Shelf Indulgence, unable to search for their favorite angel; Baba the shaman starts a new tradition to bring peace to the town; as a human among a family of witch hunters and surrounded by supernaturals, Brock Blackstone questions if he'll ever find love; Cece the angel tries to figure out why a tourist creates a trail of anger and darkness in his wake; Shade the reaper must prove his loyalty to Death or lose his love and life in Havenwood Falls forever; Addie Beaumont faces huge life changes that could shift the entire power dynamics of the town; Infiniti learns to find her own peace when a blizzard hits Havenwood Falls; Mike McCabe tries to stay calm while preparing for Christmas Eve festivities while the blizzard threatens his daughters' lives; and Cat Vega and Dingane decide where they're going with their unlikely relationship.

These short stories are all about love, friends, and family, centered on the theme of peace, brought to you by *USA Today* and Amazon bestselling and award-winning authors in the Havenwood Falls Collective.

Authors in this anthology include:
T.V. Hahn
Belinda Boring
Nadirah Foxx
Morgan Wylie
Susan Burdorf
Justine Winter
Kristie Cook
Rose Garcia
E.J. Fechenda

DON'T MISS OUT!

Stay up to date at www.HavenwoodFalls.com

Subscribe to our reader group and receive free stories and more!

HAVENWOOD FALLS SHORT STORY ANTHOLOGY 2021

HAVENWOOD FALLS COLLECTIVE

CURSE, CROSS, CRUET AND CURE

BY T.V. HAHN

A Teeny Weeny Tahini Thanksgiving Story

*T*hank the goddesses that my Tell All Ball revealed the warning in time for me to notify the mayor. It was just a few days before Thanksgiving as I hurried to her house shortly after the crack of dawn to give her the dreadful news. I hadn't even bothered to text her 911 to let her know I was coming over pronto!

Mayor Barbie, all six feet of her, was already dressed for the day and expertly made up, her bright red lipstick matching the red highlights mixed in a field of her green cotton candy-like bouffant hairdo. She was certainly prepared for the upcoming Christmas events, which would follow our Thanksgiving celebrations.

She could tell I was either excited or nervous by the way I was hopping around on one foot then the other, but the grimace on her face indicated that she suspected it was the latter. She grabbed my hand and pulled me quickly through her front door, and slammed it shut behind us.

1

"What in the world has you so upset, Siobhan?" She was one of the few who called me by my given name, rather than either of the public ones, Madame Tahini or Teeny Weeny.

I told her what the swirling lights of the Tell All Ball exhibited to me as I sipped my morning tea.

"A curse?" she gasped. "On one of our beautiful Havenwood Falls trees? Which one? Who placed the curse?"

I explained to her that I hadn't identified the tree yet, nor the creator of the cruel curse, but that if any harm came to that particular tree, a plague would be released and infect all the residents of Havenwood Falls.

"Well then, I will have to declare a moratorium on any tree cutting until you have been able to determine at least which tree has been chosen as the host of such a vicious virus." She gave a little smile, silently congratulating herself on coming up with the alliteration for my benefit, but not long as the occasion did not call for it. "Make sure you post the Moratorium notice on the town's website. The citizens will not be too happy about not being able to cut down their holiday tree right after Turkey Day. Hopefully, you will be able to find the answers in time for our dear lumberjacks to glean their trees. I'll alert the town council and the Court to get the word out to as many people as possible, especially the ones they know have been grinding their axes."

Okay, even I had to let out a little giggle on that joke. I let her know I would start studying my books to find the right potion to cure the tree tampered with by some vile vermin and beckon the Ball to find the pine, and I left to skitter across the square back to my town home marked with the sign that now read: *Madame Tahini's and Master Wu's Potions, Lotions, Palm Readings and Other Extra-Sensory Services.*

As soon as I got back home, Tang, the love of my life, greeted me with a warming cup of Dragon Well Green Tea, his specialty and my new favorite. He removed my cloak from my shoulders and hung it upon the hook in the foyer.

I gave him a quick peck on the cheek and told him about the work I had to do today. He politely told me he would stay out of my way, since he already had plans to meet Mat and Nina at Coffee Haven for scones and coffee, then Nina was going to take him to pick out a turkey, something Mat of course was not too keen on, being an owl shifter and all. Tang would have her show him how to prepare it, so he could make dinner on Thanksgiving Day.

It's no wunder why I love the Wu.

Ducking into my salon, I went directly to the drop-down desk to log into the password-protected website. I was not going to change the password this time, but to post the Moratorium news, as big and bold as my fonts allowed. I didn't want any of our townsfolk to miss this, so changing the password at this time would be a big mistake.

Then I perused the large bookcase that took up the entire back wall of the room. I found just the right book, my go-to choice, so to speak. The HOHUM book, which of course there was nothing ho-hum about it. It stood for *Handbook Of Healing Unctions & Mixes*. I wheeled my librarians ladder over to where the green covered book poked out of the top shelf and climbed up the steps to grab it. As if it knew what I was after, the book seemed to leap out of my hands and fell directly onto the top of the round table, next to my glass ball of wisdom and revelation.

Of course, as was its nature, the book had fallen open to page 77, a recipe for a remedy for whatever a plant may pale. The ingredients read as follows:

- *Amazonite crystal*
- *A cruet of charmed water*

- *4 pure white hairs of a Tibetan creature*
- *A light from an ethereal fire*

I knew exactly where to find these items, but I did not have the time. I would set the pixie sisters out to gather them up for me and pray they would be back before nightfall, but it would give me the reprieve I needed to work with my ball and sky charts in order to find evidence of the evergreen affected by this evil curse.

I was about to text Tang to ask him to walk up the path into the forest, to Cyllene's home, the once famous Maximus, a giant Bristlecone Pine that had a stroke of misfortune when struck by lightning. Cyllene was the soul of Maximus, his tree nymph, who basically looked like an eerie iridescent gypsy moth but with powers, and my closest long-time friend. But, as closest long-time friends do, Cyllene made her appearance right outside my kitchen window.

She used to just tap at the window, but that really only worked if I was in the kitchen. Tang came up with the ingenious engineering of hanging a small bell that she could tap, but the decibels of that bell would be able to reach my sensitive ears throughout my abode.

"Silly Annie, what perfect timing!"

She flew immediately to a clever contraption that Tang invented for our communication to replace the old tongs and funnel setup that we had used to amplify Cyllene's chatter.

"First off, it's Cyllene, pronounced see-lee-knee."

"Yeah, whatever. It's great to see you! I need your help. I need you to round up the pixie sisters. I have a few items I need them to gather before Christmas and Havenwood Falls are doomed."

The illustrious oread never had a chance to fly off to find the pixies, since as soon as I finished speaking, the four imps came tumbling through the kitchen window, falling on top of one another, which immediately turned into a wrestling match across the wooden planked floor.

"Enough! I need your help, girls!"

Other than maybe wrestling one another, I believed the pixies liked "helping" me more than anything else, along with bringing me colored ribbons of course.

They halted their grappling and stood at attention, hilariously saluting me and looking like a box of toy tin soldiers dressed in skirts.

"This is of utmost and urgent importance! I need you four to collect some items for a recipe that I need to concoct to cure a conifer and save our town. You girls will be instrumental in this rescue, so I want you to pay close attention."

Their eyes opened even wider than they already were as they simultaneously lowered their salute but remained at attention.

"You must all stay together. Cyllene will accompany you on this mission and will remember each of the steps you need to take so follow her lead."

One of Cyllene's special talents was a powerful memory. I supposed that came from the thousand or so years of being the soul of Maximus. Even in her fading years, she still had remarkable retention.

"Tierri, you must collect some amazonite. These are crystals that you should be able to find at the old mine at the base of where Mount Alexa and Mount Sousa meet. There is a rockslide inside. Use your earth gift to mine out the mineral.

"From there, you are all to go up to Peacock Lake. Ushka, here is a cruet you will need to carry some water from the lake. Although probably as a pixie you are safe from the potentially poisonous qualities of the lake, I think it is best for you to call Coralie with the siren's song, and she will fill the cruet for you."

We'd brought Coralie, a mermaid, from my homeland, the

Isle of Gwyn'fl, to reunite her with my brother Grenfold, her only true love, and she his.

Ushka graciously accepted the cruet and stopper then asked me to repeat the siren's song.

"Of emerald eye and ruby hair, Enchantress of the Sea. Of sweetest song and purest heart, Please come our Coralie."

Ushka bobbed her head up and down enthusiastically, as the other sprites said they would help her remember the song. I hoped between the four of them they could get it right. Cyllene suggested, as if reading my mind, which I think she could, that each of the pixies remember a part of the verse.

"Great idea!" I agreed. "Tierri, you remember 'Of emerald eye and ruby hair.' Enya, you remember 'Enchantress of the Sea.' Aeiri, you remember 'Of sweetest song and purest heart.' And Ushka, take the last line and remember 'Please come, our Coralie.'"

Each of them began singing the stanza assigned to them. I let it go for about three or four rounds to help it embed in their memory before calling an end to the ruckus.

"There is still more to collect. After you get the water from the lake, you all then need to go to see HimaLaLa."

That started a new wave of excitement, each jabbing one another while jumping up and down. At this rate, Christmas will have come and gone.

I handed Aeiri a bag of cookies to give to HimaLaLa, the wayward yeti that lost its way into Havenwood Falls and has been residing in Gruff's old cave, since Gruff the troll was turned back into his fae form of Grenfold and joined Coralie in Peacock Lake.

"Aeiri, I need you to pluck four long hairs from HimaLaLa's back. Your sisters can keep him distracted with the cookies."

I made sure the bag was chockful of daisy flour cookies, as the sisters were as likely to eat them up faster than the Yeti and before Aeiri had finished her pruning.

"Lastly, you will all need to make your way up to my cabin. Enya, you need to retrieve the lantern in my chest. It is the one that is made up of prisms. Here is the key to the cabin. The chest is unlocked."

Enya anxiously wrapped her hot little hands around the key, then popped it into her pocket.

I made a special list for them, made of images of each of the items they needed to collect, and handed it to Tierri for safe keeping, she being the most grounded and reliable of the bunch.

"One last thing! A warning!"

All four of them went back to their attention-standing position, aware that warnings were not to be ignored.

"Do not harm any trees in the forest, not even breaking a twig! It could possibly injure the entire town."

A collective gasp issued from the line of little fae.

"That means no rough housing when in the woods. Okay, now hurry! I need you back before dark."

And with that, they scampered off with Cyllene flying as quickly as she could to get in front of the pixie pack.

I spent the rest of the morning in my salon, combing through maps and surveys and charts of all sorts, trying to determine at least the area of the cursed conifer. Also, constantly referring to a tremendously voluminous volume of the trees of the canyon itself.

At the same time, I kept beseeching the ball to explore all the trees of Havenwood Falls that may have become ill-fated.

Around mid-afternoon, I realized I was still in my robe and slippers, which reminded me that I went to Barbie's this morning dressed like this. No wonder she was not surprised that I was nervous and anxious.

I took a break to go upstairs to my room to get dressed, fix my hair, and brush my teeth. While I stood in front of the open wardrobe, wondering what to wear, which seemed always to be the hardest decision of my day, I heard the front door close. Ah, Tang must be home, so I quickly fetched what was right in front of me and finished my grooming before returning downstairs to greet him.

Instead of Tang, it was Mat, my nephew. The huge hulk of a handsome hunk picked me up right off the floor and hugged me hello.

"And it's good to see you too, Mat. How are Nina and Tang doing with the turkey hunt?"

"They selected the perfect sized turkey, and Nina was just reviewing the cooking instructions when I left. She's going to fix Coniglio all' Anconetana for me," he replied with a wide smile, proud of his Italian, which Nina had been teaching him for the past few years.

"Conig...what?"

"It's stuffed rabbit, but don't tell the pixie sisters that it's rabbit. It tastes just like turkey."

I laughed but had to ask him how in the world did he know what turkey tasted like.

"I've had a few squabbles with those gobblers in the past," he answered with a wink.

"Make yourself at home. You can light a fire in the parlor for me, if you'd like. I've got a lot of research to do."

An hour or so passed when my Tell All Ball lit up like a firecracker and spewed colored lights all over the salon from floor to ceiling. Eureka, it found something! I gazed into its blessed roundness only to become dismayed. The vision in the sphere showed the stand of Bristlecone Pines that surrounded my cabin in the mountains. The same cabin the boisterous brownies were heading to last.

I crossed my fingers and prayed to the goddess Brid to protect my trees and keep the imps a safe distance from the stand. Unfortunately, the Ball was unable to determine which of the trees in the stand had been infected, but there were only ten, so again I crossed my fingers and prayed that there would be enough potion to attend to all of them.

I dialed 911 on my cell, my direct line to the mayor to let her know that I had at least identified the area and that she could lift the Moratorium with the warning that anything west of Peacock Lake was off limits.

"Thank goodness! My phone has been ringing off the hook with complaints from timberers in a tirade." I could almost hear her little smile over the phone. "I'll let the town's council and the Court know, and you post the good news."

I went back to my computer and typed "CHRISTMAS TREE MORATORIUM LIFTED" but included the cutting caution with exclamation points, lots of them and underlined. "HOWEVER, MORATORIUM STILL IN PLACE FOR ANY TREE WEST OF PEACOCK LAKE !!!!!!!!!!!!!"

I no sooner finished my post when Tang appeared with the turkey, and I led him into the kitchen where he placed it on the counter between the sink and the oven.

I gave him the news about locating the stand of trees that hovered over my cabin.

An intense look came across his face as he pondered this revelation. "Siobhan, I think I may know who placed this curse. Sometimes forgiveness does not change a person. It sounds like the work of Mai Li."

Ah, Mai Li, the sorceress scorned by Tang and forgiven by both of us.

"She could transcend time and space to wrought this rot?"

"I believe she has the knowledge to place a curse that would follow either you or me. Since the stand is so close to your A-frame, I believe she set it on you."

I slumped over in despair. Now what? Anywhere I went I could conceivably wreak havoc?

"If we cure this plague, can she do it again another time?"

"If I'm correct about the curse, yes. However, there may be

a way to cast a spell that would protect Havenwood Falls from befalling her curses ever again."

"That would be wonderful, Wu! Meanwhile, what do you need for your spell?"

"I believe I saw an ancient Chinese puzzle box at Callie's Consignments a month or so ago. I hope it is still there. I will most likely need your help to use your wand to complete the spell and enter the portal back to Tiger Pond in 3519."

"That sounds so dangerous, Tang. Promise me you will be careful and come home safely!"

"I'll do my best, my Teeny Weeny *Xiānnǚ*."

The sky was beginning to darken, and it was evident that the news of the lifted ban had spread like wildfire by the sounds of the teens honking their horns as they paraded in their cars around the square. Or maybe it was just the fact they'd been released from their confining classrooms for the long holiday weekend.

Mat slumbered blissfully in the overstuffed chair by the comfort of the raging fire in the hearth.

Tang and I finished straightening up the salon, but I was doing my hopping dance, nervously waiting for the pixies to arrive, when I heard the chime of a distant bell penetrating my ear drums. I flinched at the sound. Then changed my dance to excitedly anticipating their arrival.

"What is it, my love?" Tang asked.

"Cyllene is back! The bell you created just rang." He was right. It was a "deci-bell" that only I could hear.

I flew open the kitchen window sash to admit my beloved crew.

Sure enough, according to Cyllene, their adventure was indeed delayed by many outbreaks of arguing, such as which rockslide to mine and who was supposed to sing which verse first, second, third, and fourth—not that they could count. Then of course there was plenty of wrestling, jabbing, rolling over with laughter, and trying to lick up every cookie crumb that could be had in HimaLaLa's cave. She also told me that wherever there were trees, she used the swallow tail of her wings to draw crosses in the snow. Oddly, the pixies understood that mean no trespassing. She wasn't sure why she drew crosses, except she felt something from me about crossed fingers, so she gave it a whirl.

The pixies unloaded their haul onto the kitchen table then ran straight to the parlor to embed themselves into Mat's bulked body and fell fast asleep.

Alas, another reprieve. Tang and I just hugged and smiled.

I told Cyllene I had one last request for her. I could tell she was exhausted, but she was always eager to please me. How fortunate I was.

I explained that I needed her to light the prism lantern, as I was sure the ethereal light mentioned in the book would be a combination of the nymph's glorious flame and the chromatic rays that would emit from the lantern.

I opened the top of the lantern that sat on the table, and Cyllene did her exquisite dance above the beacon, begging for her enlightenment.

"Next time, we dance together, my dearest friend!"

She nodded, knowing I would effervesce, and we could do-si-do together.

I waved as she flew out of the window and back to her mate Maximus, then closed the window to shut out the chill wind that had begun to whip up behind her exit.

I gazed upon my rather tiny kitchen, now adorned with a turkey and other items absconding my kitchen table, with a weariness I had forgotten I possessed since before dusk.

Unfortunately, gathering ingredients does not a potion make, so there was still work to be done.

Tang removed the turkey from the counter by finding the perfect pot to set it in to brine. Then he carefully pushed my "ingredients" to the side. Not a word was spoken between us. He just saw the weariness in my eyes, but he knew I had the fortitude to venture forward.

I went back to the salon and reviewed the instructions in *HOHUM*, so I could create the formula correctly.

> *Instructions as follows:*
> *Crush the amazonite crystal with a mortar and pestle*
> *Put the crushed mineral into a cast iron pot*
> *Add 10 droplets of charmed water*
> *Take 4 white hairs and dice.*
> *Mix all over a heated plate*
> *When near to boiling pass the ethereal light over the pot*
> *Mixture should bubble and squeak. When it does it is ready.*

That was it? Ready for what? Oh, my Goddesses! First, how was I supposed to crush a hard rock with a mere mortar and pestle? Second, and more worrisome, I couldn't touch iron. How could I even work with an iron pot? Iron was extremely toxic to me and all fae. I thought I could do this, but I couldn't.

It was hard to admit, but at this point, aside from the weariness, I just broke down in tears.

"My *Xiānnǚ*?" is all Wu said, then wrapped the most loving arms around me and peered over my shoulders as he read the instructions in the book behind me.

"Say no more! Don't you realize we are a team, a family! Everyone works together. If nothing else, my dearest, you taught me that. I will handle the pot. You are the one who understands the rest. Use your faerie magic."

Again, Brid and all the heavens had blessed me.

I got to work. Tang had made all the space for me. I grabbed my green marble mortar and pestle and picked up the rocks Tierri had mined.

To my amazement, there were at least ten crystals in the rock she delivered. Don't underestimate that little one's ability. I only needed to crush one, so I scrubbed off the mud, and pulled out a chisel to chop off a loose piece. Along with the amazonite was some smoky quartz, and I added what I didn't use to my stash of gems under the sink.

After crushing the crystal, done more by faerie magic than by the pestle itself, I stepped far away as my sweetheart brought the iron pot in and placed it on the stove. I wasn't sure where he procured it from, but I guessed from Nina, though it mattered not. He would be in charge of the pot.

I handed him the mortar filled with the crushed amazonite, and he tossed it into the pot.

"Tang, it calls for ten droplets of the charmed water. I have an entire cruet. Droplets are completely different from drops. I need the eyedropper."

Tang opened a drawer next to the sink and pulled out the eyedropper. Enya apparently had woken up before the others and popped up at the same time we were supposed to do the drops. Startled, Tang dropped the dropper. It crashed into a pizillion* pieces on the floor. (*see Teeny Weeny footnote). His face had such a look of forlornness, as if he believed he had messed this all up.

"No sweat, sweetie, there's a glass tube in the same drawer and will accomplish the same thing. I can handle that part," I offered, and his demeanor changed back to the man I knew and loved.

Reaching into the drawer, I withdrew a slim line of glass tubing, approximately the same size as the eyedropper's tube. So again, I crossed my fingers and sent praises to my matron goddess Brid to let my fingers act as the suction for this tube in the perfect proportions.

I set the glass tube atop the cruet of water and withdrew what I hoped was ten droplets. Then I crossed fingers on both hands and prayed again.

I glanced over the kitchen table to find the yeti hairs. Again, thank the heavens for our family. The pixie sisters had kept HimaLaLa so happy. They gave him some of the cookies then they danced, sang wrestled, and basically entertained their buddy and cave mate, HimaLaLa. Oddly, so much so that Aeiri was able to pluck ten hairs, not just four, from the beautiful beast.

Since at this point I was hoping to create a cure that would cover ten trees, not just one, I was apprehensively hopeful that my darling dimpled imps in their exuberance to please me had awarded us with enough ingredients to actually cure the entire strand, and the lantern lit by Cyllene's fabulous flame would stay lit long enough to hatch this batch of balm for my bristlecone stand.

This strange mix of friends, family, and foreigners just may be able to fix this.

As the batch was brewing to a boil, I took the lantern still lit, albeit waning, and passed it over the pot. Then I stepped back to wait for the bubble and squeak. I looked around for Tang, but he was no longer in the kitchen. I called out for him but there was no response.

I began to freak out. I needed him to remove the pot from the stove and to help ladle it into a suitable container. It could easily overcook and be ruined.

I stood over the steaming stew saying repeatedly, "Don't squeak! Don't squeak!"

"Well, all right already, I won't make a peep," whispered my dearest Wu.

"Oh, my heavens, where were you? Don't answer! No time! I need you to be ready to transfer the cure into a jar or something as soon as it squeaks."

I handed him the ladle and began fumbling around in the cupboard for a container. I came across a wide-mouthed crock with a lid and handle. It would be perfect. I set it next to the stove just as the pot of potion squeaked, and I squealed, "It's ready!"

Without wasting any time, Tang sidled up next to me and began ladling the potion into the earthen crock. Once it was full, I capped it right away, not to take any chance that even a tiny bit may evaporate.

"Whew! Sorry about that, Tang. Thank you for coming to my rescue, but where did you go?"

He explained that he ducked out for just a minute to see if Callie's Consignment was still open. As luck would have it, Callie's cousin Nikita was just getting ready to lock up. She knew the box he was looking for, and again, good fortune smiled on us, as it had not yet sold.

"I told Nikita that I was in a hurry, so she let me take it and said we could settle up after the holiday. She had plenty to do herself in preparations. I guess there's a reason this holiday is all about thankfulness."

I then just noticed he set a package on the table. I opened it up, and inside was an exquisitely decorated box designed with dragons of all sorts on all sides in ivory and pearl. I tried to open it but could make no sense of how it worked.

Tang just smiled, removed the box from my hand, and with a few twists and another few turns, the lid popped open.

"As I said, it's a Chinese puzzle box. One needs to know the secret combination in order to open it. If I cast it with the right spell, I will be able to trap Mai Li in the box. We will then need to have the enchanted entrapment secured for eternity."

"I think Addie Beaumont can assist us in that endeavor. She can send it to the Infernum, never to be seen on this earth ever again."

"Then first thing in the morning, you take my wand and push through the portal, and I will take my potion to paint the pines in the stand."

Wu awoke before me, and I found him staring at my wardrobe in wonderment.

"So the portal back to my homeland and time is in this piece of furniture?" he queried.

"Yes, so to speak. I will have to create its opening with my wand, but you will need your compass to get there and, of course, home again!"

Master Wu, as always, was prepared, the Chinese Puzzle Box in one hand and the Come Home Compass in the other. He had donned his more ancient clothing, ready to fit in with the time and place he was headed.

He nodded, and that was my cue to open the portal (and pray a lot). I touched my wand to the tip of my nose, then tapped the wardrobe. A large glowing amaranthine colored hole appeared in the side of the wardrobe, and right before Tang walked into it, he wrapped his arms around me, still securing his treasured tools, and kissed me full on the lips.

My fingers, lobes, nose, and toes began to tingle so I quickly pushed him through the portal, before I could have any second thoughts and ended up begging him to stay.

Now, it was my turn to handle the Havenwood Falls side of the curse. I dressed quickly, grabbing my warmest coat before heading to the kitchen to carry the crock of the curative concoction to the cabin in the woods.

Tierri had thoughtfully left the key to the cabin on the table next to the container. I slipped the key into my coat pocket, grabbed the handle of the container, and stepped out the kitchen door into my backyard.

The most expedient way for me to travel to my secluded sylvan sanctuary was to shimmer. The air around me vacillated as I slipped into the ripple.

When I arrived outside the cabin, I noted that the sun was nearly at high noon. *Ah, that darn stipple in the ripple.* A light dusting of snow had covered the steps leading to the door as I stepped up to it and fit the key into the lock.

Wasting no time, I immediately went to the chest at the back of the cabin and rummaged through it until I found a large, wide paintbrush. Now completely armed, I set about my task of painting the greenish turquoise potion upon the tainted pines. I took Cyllene's cue and used brush strokes that formed a cross on every tree, including their roots, while begging my Goddess Brid to protect them all.

Now having completed the chore, I washed up the paintbrush and crock, returned the brush to the chest, and locked up the cabin, then shimmered home again.

I arrived just as the sun was beginning to set, even though it seemed I had only left my house about an hour and half ago.

Tang was waiting for me in the kitchen, a huge smile on his face, a seemingly rather noisy puzzle box on the table, and dancing lights in his hair. The last being a side effect from traveling through my portal.

I told him about painting the crosses on the ten trees. He nodded and fingered a symbol similar to the one now adorned on each of my saplings.

"That is the Chinese symbol, shi, which is the number ten. You have ten trees, Tierri brought you ten amazonite crystals, and you needed ten droplets of water. Rather prophetic, I would say."

"And apparently I'd been gone for ten hours."

We both laughed as we pondered the power of ten.

The two of us straightened up the kitchen from the harried day before. I pointed to the raging riotous puzzle box and motioned to Tang to place it in the iron pot and move it to the back of the pantry, in hopes that no one would accidentally or otherwise find it. He patiently abided me, but he did not realize that my sensitive ears could hear the trapped woman screeching and screaming. Fortunately for me, it was in her native tongue, so I could not understand her words, but it sounded clearly to me that her raging rants were of a very venomous nature.

The table cleared off, Tang put the new leaf that he had fashioned into its place, and I began to set the table for our Thanksgiving dinner. Normally, the holiday meal would be more like a supper, somewhere around four in the afternoon. However, we had taken to having tea about then since Tang had fallen for the English custom, so dinner tended to occur just a bit later. It worked well with me because I liked tea, and Michaela tended to do an afternoon tea at Whisper Falls Inn.

I laid down the Thanksgiving tablecloth that the talented Nina had made for the newly extended table and arranged our plates, napkins, and flatware in preparation. Nina had also made a smaller version to cover the parlor table (the "children's table" during holidays) for the pixies. Plates were the only thing required for the incorrigible imps. Napkins and flatware were possibly dangerous if in their possession.

Once Nina and Mat were married, then Tang and I, it was evident that my little family was growing and that not only the table had become extended. As much as it hurt in some way that the pixies and I (and even Mat at one time) no longer spent this holiday with my best friend, Barbie—whose spread for the feast at the mayor's mansion could not be matched by any in the canyon—I was ever thankful to have my very own family Thanksgiving.

Early in the morning, both Tang and I began cooking the Festival Feast.

I was setting up to prepare the vegetables, while Tang was chopping away to create our stuffing. I glanced over and saw that he was chopping hazelnuts, pine nuts, and even some black walnuts.

I screamed out, "WHAT ARE YOU DOING??"

Really, yelling was not my mantra, in any way, shape or form. In fact, it was totally unlike me. I was not sure where this was coming from, but thankfully I realized I over-reacted and toned down my response.

"My sweetest, don't you know that Nina is allergic to peanuts? We cannot add that to the stuffing or she will start puffing!"

Tang Wu stepped back, regarded the situation, and then continued chopping.

"Did you not hear me?"

"Loud and clear, my Teeny Weeny fae. But a peanut is not a nut. Granted, you can find plenty of nuts in Havenwood Falls, but your peanut is not one of them. It's a seed from the pod of a legume. Nuts come from trees. Peanuts are no different than any other legume other than it's a strange breed that grows underground like a tuber. However, they are the seeds of a pod, like your sweet peas, even a snow pea is a pod that protects its seeds, or a soy bean that produces your favorite edamame. It is not that a nut is not a seed, ubt its properties are different. Besides, I actually went over these ingredients with Nina when she was giving me the instructions on preparations. In fact, some of these are actually in her rabbit recipe."

The turkey was stuffed and trussed and tossed into the oven to roast. Then Tang and I started on the traditional trimmings of cranberry sauce, mashed potatoes, sweet potato casserole, green beans, and a few sidekicks such as my favorite black olives.

Nina and Mat appeared at the house right about five o'clock, carrying a well adorned roast rabbit on a platter. Tang had already started carving the turkey and Mat the rabbit. We laid out the feast on the kitchen counter, basically using it as a buffet table.

The pixies, as fervently ravenous as little people can be (which is truly scary), started filling their tiny bowls with whatever was on the counter. The Coniglio all' Anconetana included. as we had cut the rabbit delicacy into a few smaller pieces for them to try.

Tierri, as no surprise, asked what this dish was, pointing to the unfamiliar platter. Nina told Tierri that this was a traditional Italian "Thanksgiving" dish. There were no turkeys in the part of Italy that she came from, but this was pretty dang close to what they served for their harvest thankful feast.

"We made a special platter for all of you to try. Even a little stuffing. which includes my homeland's pignoli."

I could not be more grateful for all the souls in my life.

1 & 2) Cyllene and Barbie—my truest and best friends.

3, 4, 5 & 6) (since I am counting)—my sweetest little worker bees: Aeiri, Enya, Tierri, and Ushka (worker bees on some days, sort of, however, this time absolutely, and they of course are quite the mix of pix).

7 & 8)—that's for Mat and his mate Nina. They met because of me and turned out to be a magnificent match.

9) All the wonderful residents of Havenwood Falls.

10) TANG, because he is a TEN, and my number ONE. I had no idea how I was so fortunate to fall in love with Tang Wu and him with me under the most grueling and vigorous battles. However, that had proven to be one of the best moves I had ever made in my life.

With him—with all of my family gathered here—I'd found true peace.

Nina, Mat, Tang, and I sat at the extended table with our respective delicacies, each to his or her own liking.

Shortly after we finished grace, we heard some delighted squeals emanating from the parlor that sounded much like "This tastes like Turkey!"

Happy Thanksgiving from Madame Tahini, Wu & the Crew

*Teeny Weeny footnote: Pizillion can only refer to broken glass. It doesn't matter if it is a small juice glass, a wine glass, or an elaborate decanter. It can also be a window, a Tiffany lamp shade, a lantern. And as I've witnessed through so many centuries, glass obelisks of enormous proportions shatter into a pizillion pieces. Like the grains of sand the glass is made from, it is impossible to count, and its bitsy shards of the broken item continue to show up for an eternity. Pizillion!

Have you read all of Madame Tahini's tales by T.V. Hahn?
The Winged & the Wicked
The Ward & the Wanderers
The Wu & the Wand

OPERATION GRINCH

BY BELINDA BORING

A Shelf Indulgence Christmas Story

*D*eck the halls with boughs of Holly . . .

I softly hummed along to the Christmas carol playing over the store's speakers. I couldn't help but sing the last part dramatically, emphasizing my name that ended the first line. It was my thing with Micah for as long as I could remember. This year, every melodic note that filled the air symbolized the small victory Sedona and I had won over Havenwood Falls's resident Grinch. Or, at least, that's what we called Micah when he scoffed at our desire to get into the festive spirit shortly after Halloween was over. Something about giving Thanksgiving a chance to shine before we brought out the glittering tinsel, baubles, and twinkly lights.

Sedona had looked at him incredulously.

I silently counted down the seconds before he caved in defeat. He had no problem standing strong against me . . . His beloved empath, however? He was putty in her hands.

It made for great entertainment.

Shelf Indulgence, the town's favorite bookstore, was her domain, and in an act of compromise, Sedona declared we would keep the home decorations to a minimum but that Micah, my guardian, had zero say in what she did within her business.

Hence, the fact that we'd been singing along to holiday music since November 1st.

I made sure to turn the volume up and be as obnoxious as possible whenever he was in the store. Sedona didn't even hide her smirk and amusement at his discomfort.

He asked for it.

Who the hell didn't love Christmas?

Which brought me back to the task at hand . . . my secret project for our new family tradition. Last week during dinner, Micah had confessed that perhaps it was time for him to join in on the *insanity*—his word for what he often teased was our festive obsession—and start something new this year. The only clue he would give us was that it was tree related, and that got me thinking.

We lived in a magical town.

Most of my friends were magical.

Heck, my guardian was a genuine angel who had sworn an oath to keep me hidden and protected from those who would want to hurt me for my oracle powers. We'd come to Havenwood Falls seeking refuge, and in the process, he'd fallen in love with Sedona, an empathic witch who was not only one of my closest friends, but someone I secretly looked at as a mother figure.

Magic surrounded me and infused every aspect of my daily life.

Magic ran through my veins, even though I wasn't allowed to access it—enemies and all.

But that didn't stop me from longing to touch the power that tingled with electricity beneath my skin and whispered with power.

Use me.

Set me free.

Like an obedient daughter, I ignored the forbidden lure and pulse. I trusted Micah with my life, and I'd seen the fear that filled his eyes through the years whenever a threat would get too close.

I shook my head, letting thoughts of the past tumble away. It was finally December, and I had a Christmas idea that kind of pushed the magical boundaries Micah had set—that basically I never tap into my own. I'd found a book here in Shelf Indulgence . . . *Magical Enchantments for the Modern Witch.*

Sedona had snorted when the book arrived in the last shipment. Flicking through the pages, she'd mentioned how diluted and weak the spells were, making it a perfect gift for the human residents and tourists. Magic and the mystic excited mankind like they were flirting with the dark side. Little did they know how close they tangled with the real thing.

They'd probably pee their pants, I mused, smirking, flipping through the same book now. *That, or run for the hills screaming.*

It was easy to be brave when the truth was hidden.

The spell that had caught my eye earlier now lay open in front of me. Glancing about to make sure the store was still empty of customers and that Sedona hadn't snuck back through the door while I was distracted, I ran my finger over the page, mouthing the words softly.

"Perfect," I exclaimed. Guilt niggled from the back of my mind. Surely this didn't really count as true magic. These enemies who had hunted me, chasing me and Micah around the world since I was born, couldn't possibly feel this tiny spell being cast, especially behind the powerful wards of Havenwood Falls. I shook my head, dismissing the thoughts.

Besides, it was Christmas, and my project was harmless.

Excitement bubbled up inside me again as I pulled out my phone to take screenshots of the spell and details. There was no way I'd risk taking the book out of the store and have to explain why I had it with me.

I was already having to come up with a plan to get the specific ingredients and then find a way to get out from my guardian's watchful eye to perform the spell.

Sometimes Micah drove me nuts with how overly protective he was. Plus having to try to keep my feelings private and away from Sedona's empathic abilities was exhausting.

They were probably both bloodhounds in past lives—sniffing relentlessly until they uncovered their prey.

Me.

I closed the book, hugging it to my chest as a smile curled my lips.

It was official. I was going to cast the spell and ask for forgiveness afterward.

Operation Grinch Micah was underway.

"Looks like it's just going to be us for dinner tonight, kiddo," Sedona chimed as she came out from the back room. Pocketing her phone, she let out a long sigh. "Micah won't be home until late. Something about wanting to surprise us." She readjusted her ponytail, tugging on her long blue and purple hair to tighten it. "Which means . . ."

I straightened on the stool I was perched on behind the store's counter. "It's my choice to pick?"

Sedona was a badass in many ways, but cooking was definitely not her forte. Not that I complained. Havenwood Falls had some of the best food. My mouth already watered.

She reached beside me for the drawer where we kept the various menus from around town. I shook my head, though.

We wouldn't need them tonight. I knew exactly what I was craving.

"I'm ordering the biggest, cheesiest, most delicious ham and pineapple pizza that Napoli's can make." I closed my eyes for a moment, imagining the bliss I always experienced taking that first glorious bite.

Best. Pizza. Ever.

Sedona grinned, already pulling out her phone so we could have it delivered. "How you can be such a heathen with your topping choices with Micah as your guardian is a mystery to me, Holly. Pineapple does not belong on a pizza. How many times do we need to have this discussion?"

There was no malice in her tone. Like she said, we had this same conversation at least once a week.

She'd complain and make fun.

I'd roll my eyes and ignore her.

She'd gag and pretend to throw up when the food arrived.

I'd make loud moans of pleasure, smacking my lips to drown out her comments.

It was our thing.

The bell over the entryway door jingled, signaling a customer. Sedona gestured she'd make our order in the back room and for me to help whoever had come.

"Don't forget an extra two servings of marinara for the garlic knots," I hollered after her. Napoli's dipping sauce was beyond the best. I always used my finger at the end to get as much of the remaining tomatoey-herby goodness because wasting even a drop was a sin.

"I seriously have the best timing ever, Eryx." A couple was approaching the counter, the woman grinning from ear to ear. "My tarot reading this morning said I could expect good things today, but I didn't realize that meant pizza." Tempest leaned over and pulled me into a tight hug. "Please tell me you haven't converted to the dark side, Holl-ster, and forsaken the pineapple." She held me at arm's length, looking me in the face.

Tempest Bell was my idol. I loved everything about the water witch and made no attempt to hide that I wanted to be her when I grew up. Including snagging myself a hot boyfriend like Eryx Strathos, the guy standing beside her. I'd overheard Sedona and Micah talk about some of the hardships the couple had gone through before finally making it official. They were both juniors at the Sun & Moon Academy college and were magical bad-asses.

I giggled. "Never! I will be true to our beloved fruit until the end of my life!"

Did I mention I loved how dramatic Tempest was, and how she encouraged me to be the same? If I could choose a sister, it would be her.

"Good. Keep the faith and don't let the haters break you." She said that last part louder, making sure Sedona heard it as she came back to the front of the store. "We shouldn't be punished because others have crappy taste buds." Eryx elbowed Tempest, earning him a semi-annoyed glare. "Well, it's true," she grumbled.

"Hey, Sedona," Eryx interrupted, wrapping his arm around his girlfriend's waist as a silent peace offering. The gesture made my heart flutter. He was always touching her softly. "We're glad you're here, because we have something for you guys."

Obviously forgiven, Tempest piped up, snatching the small package out from his hand.

"Yes!" she bubbled excitedly. "Did you guys hear about the Magic of Peace Ceremony the town's going to hold in the square this weekend?"

Sedona nodded knowingly. "Yep, Addie was in here earlier, asking me if I could have flyers here on the counter to let everyone know. It's going to be a fun night."

"Whoa," I murmured. "This looks so freaking cool."

"And wait, there's more!" Tempest gushed, emptying the rest of the package's contents onto the countertop. The prettiest stone bracelets fell onto the glass. I couldn't help it—I picked one up, brushing my thumb over the threaded blue-green crystals.

"Amazonite."

Sedona nodded, smiling. "You know your crystals." She inspected the second bracelet, leaving a third on the countertop. "What makes these special?"

I was pretty sure she already knew, but I also knew she liked giving me opportunities to share things I'd learned. Just the other week I'd been found curled up in the chair in one of the reading nooks, devouring yet another book on semi-precious gems. Everything about them fascinated me.

"Amazonite is a variety of feldspar that helps open the heart chakra," I began, reciting from memory. "It's a great tool that helps with releasing trauma, aiding creativity, and infusing peace with its soothing energies." Even now I could feel the gentle waves of compassion washing through me from the stones in my palm. "If you're someone who likes to worry, this would definitely help." I placed the bracelet back beside the others, giving the gems one last living stroke.

Sedona and Tempest beamed with pride. "Exactly! Well said."

Eryx grinned as he joined in. "Don't be surprised if you're asked to teach at the Academy in the future . . . Professor Holly."

He was teasing, but I didn't pretend that his words didn't thrill me. That would be a dream!

"It's part of the peace ceremony," Tempest gushed. "And these aren't just bracelets; they're malas, too. Count the beads. Up on campus, we've been busy helping get these ready by stringing all the beads. I've made enough of these that I could do it in my sleep." Sure enough, both she and Eryx pulled their own out of their pockets. "Cool, right?"

I nodded quickly, my brain already racing a million miles a minute. Sedona wasn't the only one who loved facts. I was already mentally typing the word *mala* into Google and falling down the rabbit hole of knowledge. Thank the Goddess for the internet.

The doorbell tinkled again, interrupting our group. Before I could look to see who it was, the heady waft of garlic and oregano smacked against my senses, eliciting an involuntary groan from me. Dinner was here.

Tempest and Eryx stayed a little longer, helping us put a dent into the feast Sedona had ordered, and the conversation hopped from topic to topic. After a while, my attention wandered to other things.

December had only begun and already it was proving to be the best one ever.

A new family tradition.

A secret magical project.

And now, a peace ceremony that was guaranteed to be one I'd always remember.

Reaching for another slice of ham and pineapple pizza, I was one hundred percent in love with my life.

Shivering with anticipation, I took a big bite and rejoined the conversation.

Thank the Goddess for predictability.

If there was one thing Colorado was known for at this time of year, it was the insane amount of snow that fell. Sure enough, as we waved goodbye to Tempest and Eryx, the air was filled with the scent of an approaching storm.

"Don't stay up all night reading, Holly," Sedona whispered, and she wrapped her arm around my shoulder. "And leave one of the lights on so Micah can find his way in the dark. Can't have him crashing into my book displays and causing a mess."

She'd texted him earlier that we'd be staying in the apartment above Shelf Indulgence because of the storm. I'm sure she added a ton of mushy stuff as well, but I tried not to think of that.

One word . . . gross.

"I promise," I answered, returning her hug. "He'll be back soon?" I knew he was still in town, but it didn't stop my nerves from fraying around the edges. I never liked when he was gone —surprise related or not.

Sedona nodded and let out an involuntary shiver as she peered out into the town square and up toward the sky. "Hopefully before he catches his death."

She wandered through the store one last time, making sure everything was in order for tomorrow before retiring upstairs. Each second that passed made the butterflies flutter harder in my stomach. Finally, the door to the stairs closed, and I could hear her trudge up to bed.

In about twenty minutes she'd be fast asleep, and my secret project could begin. I'd spent the rest of the afternoon and evening gathering the few items the spell required, and later I'd tiptoe upstairs into Sedona's magic study. It was originally her grandfather's, but she'd made it her own after his death.

Which reminded me, where was the pesky ghost?

Looking for Maxwell, I didn't see him anywhere. He was known to come and go—to where he never said, but the last thing I needed was him nosing about and ratting me out. Hopefully he would stay wherever the dead go when they're not haunting the living and give me some privacy.

I studied the clock, willing it to go faster.

Fifteen more minutes.

I lay the Christmas tree angel down before me in the center of the candle-lit circle. One thing I loved about Sedona's room was that she had a pentagram etched into the center with the wood flooring carved out to accommodate the wax pillars. It helped to ensure I had everything placed correctly, making it less nerve wracking.

Doubts had already come racing to the front of my mind, bringing along their friends Guilt and Inadequacy. My hands trembled as I stroked the glittery dress and wings of the doll, careful that my fingers didn't mess the long golden strands of hair. She wasn't the most elegant of angels, but I'd seen Sedona eye her recently at the store.

Reading the short spell once again, all I was lacking was some holiday ivy to crush and use in the enchantment. The hope was to infuse the tree topper with enough peace, goodwill, and holiday cheer that Mr. Fuddy Duddy Grinch would just switch to Team Christmas and soften his heart.

At the very least, it should make him chuckle because the angel was a little tacky with the wiring in the bright blue dress all bent and warped looking.

"Okay, Holly," I murmured softly to myself, ignoring the way my voice quivered. "The spell is so simple a human could do it. What could go wrong?" Getting up on my feet, I reached for the last ingredient—the bottle of ivy leaves the book said helped invoke the Christmas spirit but stumbled at the last moment from nerves. My hand knocked over all of the nearby glass containers, and by some miracle, I managed to catch a large jar before it crashed to the ground.

I paused, barely breathing.

The room was still, but that wasn't what made me hesitate. Listening with everything I had, I waited to see if Sedona stirred.

Stay asleep, I whispered beneath my breath. *There's nothing to worry about.* My heart thudded in my ears.

Before I completely lost my confidence, I swiped up the jar of leaves, plucking a few out and then returned to the circle. I was being an idiot by overthinking it and realized this was probably something we'd laugh about together later.

I lit the candles and began.

Clearing my thoughts, I steadied myself, crushing the leaves between my fingers. Next, using the anointing oil Sedona prepared especially for ritual work, I rubbed some along the length of the chime candle I'd chosen, next sprinkling the ivy fragments over the wax.

The angel lay beside one of my favorite pieces of quartz—a cluster that seemed to shimmer and cast rainbows beneath the flickering flame. I'd read that using the crystal would help amplify my intentions, adding a real boost to the enchantment.

Licking my lips, I uttered the spell, including the added word *peace* because that was part of the Christmas spirit:

> *Goddess, hear my plea*
> *For the top of my Christmas tree*
> *Fill this angel's heart with peace and cheer*
> *So those can feel its power near.*

The book said to repeat the incantation three times while lighting the candle. Watching as the wick caught fire, I expected to feel *something* the second the words left my mouth.

Nothing.

I closed my eyes and repeated the spell with everything I had.

I peeked through my half-closed lids.

Everything appeared the same, and maybe it was just me needing some kind of sign, but the angel seemed to glow, the wings twitching slightly.

"Get your crap together, Holly," I blurted out, disappointed that for all the power I supposedly held, I couldn't even manage a simple Muggle spell. I picked up the angel, trying to sense anything that resembled peace and goodwill.

All I felt was frustration.

I'd failed, but at least I had a Christmas tree topper to offer whatever new tradition Micah was planning, and Sedona would totally *squee* over it.

Cleaning everything up and making sure no one could tell I'd been in here, I closed the door behind me and slipped into the makeshift bed on the couch.

I didn't know about Micah, but I'd all but lost my own excitement.

The delicious smell of hot apple cider woke me up.

"Good morning, sleepy head."

All I could do was mumble and stumble in the direction of the kitchen. Sedona was already fully dressed and ready to go downstairs, which meant she'd let me sleep in. Judging by the huge plate of pancakes with sides of sausages, scrambled eggs, and toast, she was also worried about something.

Her stress usually equaled carbs.

"Not that I'm complaining," I said around a mouth full of hot, maple sausage, "but why the feast?" I speared two of the fluffiest pancakes I'd ever seen and smothered them with an ocean of syrup.

I never told Sedona this, but she had a tell when it came to lying. She'd tug on her ear before playing with a strand of hair. The exact same action she was doing now. That and looking past me to the stairs leading down to the store.

"It's Christmas! Isn't that enough reason?"

I considered challenging her answer but decided to give her a freebie. She was an empath, so there was a good chance she was on overload from something going on in the town.

There was always some kind of drama happening in Havenwood Falls.

Taking a long, deep inhale over the appley-cinnamon goodness in my cup, I yelled out to the bedroom. "Get up, lazy butt, before I eat all this food!"

There was no way in hell I'd do it, and he knew it. Didn't stop me from threatening it.

There wasn't even an attempt to refute it.

"Micah!" I yelled again, glancing at Sedona questioningly. Come to think of it, he wasn't much of a sleeper-inner. He was one of the obnoxious early birds you wanted to suffocate with a pillow because he was beyond cheery in the morning.

Sedona took a not-so-subtle sip from her own cup. "He's not here." Before I could respond, she continued, and this time I saw her blatant worry. "He didn't come home."

My brain went into instant panic mode—an old habit from years on the run. She must have seen it because I was instantly hit with a wave of calm.

"He told me he was heading out to the forest for something yesterday, so with the storm that hit overnight, he probably stayed over at the Academy until it was safe to come home. He's no doubt driving Tempest and Natalie bonkers."

I snorted. "Well, it is his superpower, after all." I paused between chewing, and leveled Sedona with a serious look. "You doing okay?" I might've been young, but even I knew there was a time for no bullshit. Whatever was going on, she had to know I was old enough to handle it.

Her lips parted. She studied me closely, then shook her head. "Occupational hazard as an empath. I'm just a little tired. I'm sure he's fine." Using her fork to cut a huge piece of pancake, Sedona crammed it into her mouth, syrup dripping from her lip.

I guess that meant the conversation was closed.

We ate in silence, and once our plates were empty, she

pushed back from the table with a sigh. "Time to open the store. Meet you down there."

I nodded.

She might have said she was okay, but the mood that followed her said differently. Maybe I needed to show her the angel now.

Let the glittery wings save the morning.

"Goddess, where the hell did you find her?" Sedona exclaimed, taking the angel from me. She held the doll up in the air, moving it about. "I swear this thing is watching me like one of those creepy Elf on the Shelf things."

Not the reaction I was hoping for, but it was a start.

"It's the same one we saw in the store window, remember? You said you were going to get it for our tree this year." I pulled the sleeves of my dark pink sweater down, so they covered my fingers like gloves. Damn, it was cold.

Snow covered the town square outside, making it more and more like a winter nightmare than winter wonderland. All I could think about was the mud that would result and the countless times I'd be falling on my butt.

She peered closer at the angel. "I know, but now that I'm holding it . . ." She shuddered. "There's something not quite right." Sedona placed the angel back on the counter and stepped back. "Micah's going to hate it, so that's a plus."

I burst out laughing. "I was secretly hoping that it would cure him of his constant Grinchness." I picked the tree topper up and set her on the shelf behind me, right next to the snow globe and tumbling Santa figurine. "I guess it's more like a punishment then."

Sedona's phone rang, and I could see the instant relief. "I bet that's him now." Yet, when she looked at the lit-up screen, her frown deepened. "Hello, Tempest? No. No, Micah isn't here. In fact, I was wondering if he'd spent the night up there on campus to avoid the snow." She half-smiled over something she heard. "I know, I know, if you're wanting to avoid the stuff, you shouldn't be in Colorado."

An uneasy feeling filled my chest, and my gaze drifted to the angel.

Hanging up, Sedona looked at me, fully letting her fear show. "He wasn't there."

"And he wasn't here."

She started keying in Micah's number. It went straight to voicemail.

Where the heck was our angel?

An hour later and we still didn't have any answers.

Sedona made a quick call to Tempest, asking her her to search the SMA campus grounds just in case Micah hadn't checked in with his favorite student and instead, spent the night holed up in his office. That seemed the most logical explanation, but it left one huge question lingering . . . why he wasn't answering his phone.

That was a huge no-no between us, which drove us nuts because Havenwood Falls wasn't known for its reliable cell signal. That's why, no matter what was happening and where we were, we *always* picked up and *never ever* turned our phones off or on silent. I could still hear Micah's many lectures where he drilled that single fact into my head. It was pretty much unforgivable.

"Maybe he dropped it somewhere or the battery died?" I offered weakly, hoping against hope that was the cause for radio silence. "He wouldn't knowingly ignore you, Sedona. He wouldn't want to face your wrath." I added that last part to encourage a smile.

I was rewarded with one, but it didn't reach her eyes.

"You know what? We're probably worrying for nothing, and it's this blasted snow that's holding him up." Sedona stood and shook herself, plastering a fake peaceful expression on her face. "Let's open the store like it's a regular day."

I nodded. "And we'll kick his butt when he eventually shows up."

"Exactly." She flipped the sign that hung at the door to the *open* side. "Just because he's not here doesn't mean we should neglect the needs of our fellow bookworms, right?"

This bravado of ours lasted all of ninety minutes and three customers later when Tempest and Eryx came bursting through the door.

"Is he here yet?" the young witch asked. "Please tell me you've heard from him."

The air within the store suddenly charged with nervous energy, and a few of the nearby book displays wobbled from the power. Sedona's magic was starting to overwhelm. I cast a quick glance at Tempest as if to warn her not to push the empath too hard and saw that she'd noticed the power surge as well.

Wrapping her arms around Sedona, Tempest lowered her voice and spoke as calmly as she could. "Sorry. You know me . . . I have a flair for the dramatic." Rubbing her hand reassuringly over Sedona's back, the younger witch continued, "I just assumed with us not finding him at the academy, that he'd finally made his way home."

Sedona shook her head, her bottom lip starting to quiver with emotions. "Nothing yet."

Eryx cleared his throat and reached for her hand, squeezing it. If I didn't already know he was a demi-god, I would've sworn he was an angel as well with his golden curls loosely hanging about his face. "Just as a precaution, I asked Professor Knox if he could scout the forest to see if he could pick up any trace of Micah."

My brows furrowed. "Even after heavy snow fall?" Seemed impossible.

Tempest's eyes brightened with hope. "Professor Knox spent a lot of time in Faery and has skills that we could only dream of. We bumped into him outside Micah's office and filled him in on the situation. He immediately volunteered."

The news brought some kind of relief to Sedona as her shoulders lowered slightly. The room's atmosphere also dropped with her magic regaining control.

"Good. Good. I've heard about Knox's abilities to find whatever he seeks. If for some reason Micah's caught out there, the professor will find him." What she didn't add was the fear that Micah was hurt. There weren't many reasons why he wouldn't use his angelic gifts to at least reach out. He'd never worry us intentionally.

Eryx and Tempest exchanged a silent look.

I knew what those glances meant. Sedona and Micah did them all the time—some weird couple telepathy thing. At least they weren't making out.

"You know what," Eryx chimed, looking our way again. "How about I go to Coffee Haven and get us all some hot drinks and ask about him? Maybe someone's seen him."

Tempest cupped the side of his face tenderly. "Perfect. Don't forget to add a second pump of peppermint mocha to mine."

He kissed her on the cheek and left on his errand. I wished I could follow him. I felt helpless just standing here when I wanted to be out there searching.

Before I could begin the inevitable argument, Tempest burst out laughing, holding her sides as she looked past us.

"What the heck is that, and why is it staring at me?" Our latest Christmas decoration had caught her attention. "Please tell me Micah hates it as much as I think he does."

Sedona's mood lightened significantly as she dragged her

gaze away from the door and back to the angel on the shelf. "He hasn't seen it yet, but I'm sure he'll have plenty to say."

Tempest picked it up, almost dropping it like it burned. "Ouch!" She sucked on her finger to soothe it. Gingerly she pushed the angel back and stepped away. "Promise me you'll video his reaction." She shook her hand, staring down at her fingers. "Can Christmas tree angels bite because I swear this one almost drew blood." Sure enough, there was a red mark on her index fingertip.

"You'd have to ask Holly. She's responsible for that thing." Sedona laughed and peered closer, her frown deepening. "There's something unnerving about this doll. I just can't figure it out." She tilted her head, the loose strands of her hair falling from her shoulder. The wings began twitching again under her scrutiny. "Maybe it'll come to life and murder us all in our sleep . . ."

They both jumped when I clapped my hands. "Quit hating on my angel, please. I happened to think she's glorious."

I might've said the words, but I realized what she truly was —a reminder of my failure. The cursed thing wasn't emitting any kind of peaceful cheer at all.

"Let's get to work, shall we?" Sedona said once she stopped looking at the doll. "If I don't keep myself occupied, my magic is going to do more than mess with that thing."

So, she'd noticed the wings as well.

Angel forgotten again, the three of us settled in, waiting for the next customer and Eryx to return with our drinks.

It was early afternoon when I couldn't take the strained silence a second longer.

We'd all struggled to stay positive but there was no shaking the growing dread building inside me. I'd even turned the stupid angel around to face the wall, threatening to stuff it in the trash because the spell didn't work. I hated it.

Hovering around the register counter, Sedona and I let out heavy sighs. Tempest had escaped our somber mood earlier with Eryx, promising to call every hour for updates. Outside, the town square was bustling with people trying to navigate large snow piles and avoid stepping on black ice. Usually, we'd like to watch and see who best avoided falling, but our hearts weren't in it.

It took every ounce of willpower not to keep staring at the clock.

Another customer entered.

"Can you take care of them, Holly?" Sedona asked. She was exhausted. "I think I'm going to go upstairs and take a nap. I'm feeling beyond frazzled trying to keep myself together."

I quickly nodded, but she wasn't able to get far when we saw who'd entered.

Addie Beaumont.

Based on her expression, she wasn't bearers of good news.

"I'm gathering searching the woods was a bust." Sedona wasn't asking. She already knew the answer. She crumpled back onto the stool and buried her face in her hands. "Where is he?"

It was Addie who comforted her, patting my arm first as she passed by. "Professor Knox told me a little of what's happening when he came back from the forest. It was a long shot tracking Micah, so I also checked the town's wardings."

Sedona's head popped up, and her eyes widened. "I'd totally forgot you could do that through his tattoo." It was part of living here in Havenwood Falls that its supernatural citizens received a magical tattoo. Even I didn't remember that it meant Addie could see if Micah was still in town.

"And?" I asked, wetting my lips. "Is that why he's not here?

He left town?" Dread formed a heavy lump in my gut. It didn't bode well if he'd gone without saying anything.

Addie's eyes filled with sympathy. "He's still here. He hasn't crossed the boundaries so that at least narrows the area to search in." She looked to Sedona. "How can I help?"

We all looked to Sedona. Her brow was creased with concentration. "The only thing I haven't tried is a locator spell because I was positive he'd be home before I needed to." It was painful watching the hope she'd desperately been trying to hold on to evaporate. "I guess I was also worried that it wouldn't reveal anything."

That was the nightmare we both wanted to avoid. No response meant that Micah wasn't just missing, but possibly dead.

"He's okay, I promise," I lied. I needed to be strong for us.

She must have realized I was feeding off her emotions as well because Sedona stood a little straighter, determined. "You're right. Let's go see where he is." She gestured for us all to go upstairs. "No point waiting."

We all began to follow her, but Sedona stopped abruptly after taking a few steps.

"I can do this, Addie. I know you've got a lot on your plate with Tase."

Her friend shook her head and gestured for her to keep moving. "This is a problem I can solve, though." They exchanged a look I couldn't really interpret and figured it was one of those adult things they didn't talk about in front of kids —not that I was a child. As if changing the subject as Addie physically pushed us forward to get going, she added, "No offense, Sedona, but that angel is creeping me the hell out. Beady freaking eyes."

All we could do was laugh.

They had the ritual set up quickly, calling the guides and the guardians to protect the circle as the spell was performed. It was unspoken that I couldn't join in, so I watched from the side, enthralled.

Now *this* was what power should feel like.

The hairs on my arms rose with the energy Sedona evoked, and I secretly vowed that one day, I would be able to do the same things with my own magic. I could sense the different elements as they brushed against my body.

The grounding aroma of Earth.

The gentle breeze of Wind.

The warm embers of Fire.

The soothing coolness of Water.

The comforting assurance of Spirit.

No wonder my own spell hadn't worked.

Sedona and Addie stood in the center of the pentagram with the candles flickering and dancing about them. Sedona was holding a black tourmaline stone in her palm, a talisman to help protect her and ease her own worries. Her eyes were closed as she chanted the words to help her find Micah.

I knew the instant the incantation had worked when the crystal began hovering in the air, just above her opened hand, slowly turning about like a compass.

"Help me find him, blessed Goddess," she whispered. The serene expression she wore spoke volumes. Sedona knew her wish would be answered.

Addie looked on as well, her own hair floating away from her body. She hadn't spoken, but I knew her energy was also helping fuel the spell. This was definitely going to work.

The flames from each candle suddenly flared and grew taller and brighter.

The black tourmaline stone sped up as it continued to spin, then dropped to the ground with a crash. The loud noise surprised us all, but that was nothing compared to the hole in the wooden flooring.

Peering down through the large gap to below, Addie was the first to speak up. "Was it meant to do that?"

Sedona's eyes were wide as saucers. "Nope, but we need to go see where it went."

Quickly releasing the circle and thanking the Goddess for her intervention, we raced down the stairs, hoping to see wherever the stone had gone. I still couldn't get over how fast and hard the talisman had flown.

I gasped out loud and pointed. "Holy cow!"

Addie joined in with her own version. "Shit."

With a confused expression, Sedona closed the distance between us and where the stone was now embedded—the wall where we shelved our Christmas knick-knacks. It had swiped the angel, causing it to topple.

We all watched as the doll fell forward as if in slow motion.

Sedona screamed in pain.

"Micah!"

I whipped about expecting to see him.

Nothing.

Tears streamed down Sedona's face as she seemed to crumple inwards, wrapping her arms around her stomach in agony. "He's hurt. Oh my gosh, what's happened to him?"

She began to sway on her feet, and Addie reached Sedona first, steadying her.

"What are you feeling?" she questioned.

Sedona grimaced, struggling to speak. "I haven't been able to sense him all day until now. It's like whatever barrier he surrounds himself in disappeared, and all I can feel is his distress." She gripped Addie's arm, pulling herself toward the counter. "It's everywhere. I can't see where it ends or where it begins."

I helplessly watched, unable to do anything.

"Take a deep breath and try to ground yourself. Calm your thoughts as best as you can." With each syllable, Addie worked to bring Sedona's magic under control. "Beyond his pain . . . can you sense where Micah is?"

I could see the muscles in Sedona's jaw tense from exertion. She shook her head. "He's close. He's so close." The tremor in her voice strengthened. "He feels close enough to touch." Her fingers hovered in the air before her as though they could touch him.

She was struggling so I did the only thing I could think of. While Addie helped her, I went over to retrieve the talisman. Black tourmaline was an empath's important tool, and I couldn't help but think that if she could hold it again, maybe the stone could aide her.

No sooner had I dislodged the crystal than it yanked out of my hold and flung itself down toward the ground. It hit the angel this time, causing Sedona to scream so loud that the windows of the store rattled. There was no holding back the wave of tears that fell over her cheeks now. Her face was mottled red with pain.

I stared at her.

Then looked down at the stone embedded in the ground by my angel.

"Do that again, Holly," Addie urged, pointing to the black tourmaline. "Pick it up."

I didn't hesitate. I bent over and almost toppled forward myself from the force the stone exerted trying to escape. It struck the angel again, resulting in Sedona's howl of anguish.

The angel.

The stone was trying to strike the tree-topper.

Sedona was now curled on the floor—beyond reaching.

That's when a thought appeared, and I gagged back the sudden need to throw up.

This was my fault.

"Addie," I started, my own tears starting to fill my vision. "I think I've messed up, and I don't know how to fix it." Bending over, I picked up the angel and began to talk. I started with the book I'd found with the spell and what my intentions had been.

All I'd wanted to do was create a surprise for Sedona and a way for Micah to lighten up about Christmas. Never in my wildest dreams did I expect anyone to get hurt, and as I confessed each step I'd taken, I also shared that part of me had doubted the spell would work because it was basically for humans.

Addie listened quietly as she tried to comfort Sedona. "And it probably wouldn't have worked had a human performed it, Holly," she answered. "The thing is, you're not human, and from what Micah has disclosed, you have untapped power you're not properly trained to use."

There was the truth. It was my fault. Somehow in my ignorance, I'd turned a harmless spell into something more dangerous.

"So, what do I do?" I asked, pleading for her help to make this right. "And how did it hurt Micah?" I was frantic now. I didn't care how much trouble I was in. I just wanted everything to go back to normal.

Addie didn't say anything for a few moments. Instead, she rocked Sedona slowly, stopping only when she'd lulled her friend into an exhausted sleep. Only then did she answer. "I have a suspicion." Gently releasing Sedona, she stood, dusting off her hands. "Unfortunately, I can't have you using magic again so I'm going to need to break the spell myself."

Guilt hit me hard. "What do you need?"

Reciting a list of ingredients she needed, Addie walked over to the front door and turned the sign to *closed*, twisting the deadbolt. "When this is done, I think we're going to need to discuss the consequences to you hiding your powers and using them without supervision."

I expected as much.

Retreating back upstairs to get what Addie needed from Sedona's study, I silently vowed to never access my magic again.

That's if I survived Micah's disappointment and anger first.

If I hadn't seen it with my own eyes, I wouldn't have believed it.

Seconds after Addie had uttered the words to break my failed spell, the angel I'd enchanted had begun glowing and growing. One moment it was there, and the next, Micah stood, blood covering the sleeve of his shirt.

"Micah!" I exclaimed, rushing forward to hug him. He groaned when I collided with him, careful not to move too suddenly.

"Careful, Holly," he moaned. "I'm pretty sure something's broken." I didn't get a chance to say anything when he caught sight of his girlfriend on the ground. "Sedona!"

I would later describe what happened next like it was part of a fairytale. At the sound of his voice, Sedona's eyes popped open, as if the spell of pain she was under had broken. Relief flooded her features, and fresh tears fell.

Happy tears this time.

"Oh my gosh, you're here!" she exclaimed. Then as if by second thought, she unknowingly slapped his injured arm. "Where have you been?" She threw her arms around his neck, and he helped her stand.

"That's a good question," he replied and kissed the side of her head, holding her close. "Holly?"

He knew.

He knew I'd somehow screwed up and was responsible.

"Holly?" Sedona parroted. She looked at me, confused.

Addie cleared her throat. "I think this is a family matter, so

I'll see myself out." Before she got too far, she turned back. "Micah, we'll need to have a discussion about this later. Come find me." He nodded, and the attention turned back to me.

Where could I even begin?

Did I start with an apology first or explanation?

I jumped in with both feet. "I used magic, but I didn't think it would work, and I just wanted to cure you from being a Christmas Grinch, not hurt you, but I didn't know you'd become the actual tree topper. I'm so sorry you got hurt and that it worried Sedona because I'm such a failure, and I don't blame you if you punish me forever." My words came out as a never-ending ramble.

It was Sedona who spoke first. "You turned Micah into that creepy angel?" She looked at him. "It was you behind these beady little eyes?" The angel was back in her hands. "Crap." And with that, she started laughing. "We all commented about how much we hated it!"

"So I heard." He tried to sound gruff and hurt, but the more Sedona laughed, the harder it was for him to keep a straight face. Yet, the moment he turned to me, all seriousness returned. "I don't really know what to say to you right now, Holly. While I'm trying to understand that you meant no harm, you blatantly defied my number one rule."

"No magic," I murmured.

"No magic."

I deserved his annoyance and disappointment. I'd totally trapped him inside the doll without knowing it. I'd allowed my excitement to cloud my judgment.

Sedona remained quiet. Unlike the other times when I'd messed up, she didn't intervene or try to soften the blow. I'd broken all kids of trust.

"Go upstairs and wait for me," Micah ordered. "I'll listen to the whole story, and we'll go from there." He let go of Sedona before pulling me into his embrace. "This could've ended in disaster, sweetheart. I can't lose you."

His words gave me hope. I'd accept whatever consequences he gave me knowing that afterward, I'd earn his forgiveness.

Trudging up the stairs, leaving the two adults alone to talk, I made another wish.

That when the time finally came, I would do everything in my powers to learn and control my abilities, that I'd never find myself in this kind of situation again.

As an afterthought, a second wish surfaced . . . well, it was more of an observation.

I'd accept Micah being a Grinch about Christmas.

No tree topper, magicked or not, could ever replace the feeling of peace that having my family together brought me.

At the end of the day, I loved my angel exactly the way he was.

Have you read both of Micah and Sedona's stories by Belinda Boring?

Nowhere to Hide
Addicted to You

THE MAGIC OF PEACE

BY NADIRAH FOXX

A Baba Chapula Christmas Story

*S*omething was off that morning. The sensation disturbed me greatly. For the life of me, I couldn't figure out what was wrong. A moment later the feeling went away, and I thanked the Great One for another day. At my age, I'd learned not to give too much weight to every strange notion I experienced.

I bathed and dressed, then shuffled down to the kitchen to start breakfast. As I prepared the meal for my grandson, Hunter, and my lovely new granddaughter, Izzie, the feeling returned.

"Good morning, Baba!" Hunter rested a hand on my shoulder. "How are you today?"

A glimpse of my grandson's smiling face spoke volumes. Perhaps that was why things felt peculiar. "What news have you, Hunter?"

Before he could respond, Izzie lumbered into the kitchen

with her arms hanging by her sides. My granddaughter practically drooped, as if someone had drained all her energy.

"It's not just *his* news, Baba," she said wearily. "We're pregnant."

Why does she sound so sorrowful?

Setting the spatula on the stove, I turned to the kids. "Have you seen the doctor?"

Hunter, still grinning, placed an arm around Izzie. "She took a home pregnancy test. As soon as Dr. Underwood's office opens, we'll make an appointment."

Shouldn't Izzie be more excited? What is going on?

Before I could ask another question, Arleta, Izzie's mother, sauntered in. The female's gaze darted around the room. She briefly glanced at the slices of French toast in the skillet and then looked at me.

"Am I missing something?"

Hunter thrust out his chest and announced, "Arleta, we're pregnant!"

Izzie's mother blinked a few times before her lips curled up. "Congratulations!" Her joy quickly turned into protectiveness. "Izzie, maybe you should rest."

"Mom, I just found out. I think—"

"Nonsense. Pregnancy can be hard on Naguals. You're in a fragile state, Izzie," Arleta warned.

My granddaughter snagged a slice of bacon. "I'll be fine."

The older female scoffed. "In a year, I'll ask you how you feel."

Izzie's eyes bulged. "What happens in a year?"

"Naguals can be pregnant up to thirteen months. Plus, there's the possibility you're carrying two or more cubs. Rest while you can."

Arleta may have thought she was doing the right thing, but I sensed Izzie's unease. I touched her forearm. "Your mother's concern could be warranted. I'm fairly certain there are multiple young. My dear child, you may carry triplets."

"Triplets?" Hunter said with a gleam in his eye.

Nodding, I said, "I once heard of a female who gave birth to four cubs."

I plated the last of the French toast and handed the platter to Hunter. "Take this into the dining room. Arleta and I will be in shortly."

"Sure, Baba." My grandson intertwined his fingers with Izzie's and led her out of the kitchen.

After the kids left, I lowered my voice. "Maybe tone down the warnings, Arleta."

She flinched. "What are you talking about?"

"Telling Izzie she'll be pregnant for a year or more might have scared her."

Arleta rolled her eyes. "She deserves to know the truth. Somebody should have told me."

Before I could ask, the female grabbed the thermal carafe and sashayed from the kitchen.

I shook my head and reached for the pitcher of orange juice. When I entered the dining room, the situation grew worse. Instead of being the bearer of gloom, Arleta had done a complete one-eighty.

"I'm so glad this happened, Izzie and Hunter." Arleta poured a cup of coffee for herself and then Hunter. When Izzie nudged her cup forward, her mother said, "Oh, no, Isabel. Caffeine isn't good for the babies, or your blood pressure."

Hunter, always trying to be the neutral party between mother and daughter, said, "Arleta, surely half a cup won't hurt. We'll speak to Dr. Underwood and see what he advises."

The female said haughtily, "Nonsense. I've had my fair share of cubs. I know what's good for my daughter."

Izzie scowled and poured herself a glass of orange juice instead.

Caffeine might not be good for cubs, but neither was upsetting their mother. When Izzie found the female in a ravine outside of Havenwood Falls, Arleta claimed she'd only stay long enough to get back on her feet. A year later, she was still under Hunter and Izzie's roof. If Arleta continued her antics, she might have to leave sooner than she'd like.

Couldn't she see what her words were doing to Izzie?

Arleta said, "I doubted I'd ever have grand cubs. Oh, I can't wait to see the little gems, so I can spoil them rotten."

Izzie glared at her mother and then rose from her seat. "Spoil them? What? Like how you spoiled us? Oh, wait! You weren't there!"

"That's not—"

Thankfully, Arleta didn't finish the thought. My granddaughter ran from the room.

The outburst proved things had yet to mend between the two females.

Unfortunately, I could hear Hunter and Izzie arguing without eavesdropping. I should have walked away and given them their privacy. But listening might help me learn something worthwhile.

"I can't do this, Hunter. I'll make a terrible mother!" Her voice was so sad. Was being a parent such a miserable role for her?

"You can't possibly know that."

That's right, Hunter!

"Yes, I can! I had crappy role models. My father abandoned me and my siblings. And that shrew in the living room let us believe she was dead!"

Not exactly the word I used to describe the female.

"Your mother told us what happened. Plus, you had a grandmother who loved you."

"She shouldn't have had to raise her grandchildren."

True, but sometimes things happen.

"Izzie, the female did an outstanding job with you. You're an amazing person, despite your mother and father. You'll be—"

"Like her! Selfish. No child deserves a mother like that. I refuse to ruin another kid's life!"

Honestly, Arleta didn't ruin her daughter's life. The female closed up in that room was stronger than she believed. She could accomplish whatever she wanted.

"*Cariño*, do you plan to abandon our young?"

"No. Of course not."

That's good to know.

"Listen to me, please. Our children have nothing to worry about. Unless you plan on leaving me."

"No, I could never leave you."

"Then—"

"Hunter, I don't know the first thing about raising kids. I did a shitty job taking care of my siblings."

"I don't believe that for a minute."

"You should ask them. At times, I was too strict. Other times, I was too lenient. Most of the time, my brother and sister never listened to me."

"Izzie, you're worrying for no reason. We have plenty of time to learn everything needed to be great parents."

My grandson was right. They needed to unite, and they'd be better parents that way.

"Right, Hunter. What are we going to do? Take parenting classes?"

He laughed. "That's exactly what we'll do. We'll take as many classes as we can find. Hell, we'll get PhDs in parenting."

"Shouldn't we start with a more basic degree?"

"It doesn't matter. We will succeed. We're always stronger together. You know that, Izzie."

"We're stronger without the little ones," she said.

"And what does that mean?"

"It means we should end the pregnancy. Maybe we could get a dog to keep you company."

Hunter exploded. "What the hell, Izzie! Have you listened to anything I've said?"

"Of course I have. But—"

"But nothing! Those are my children, too. I have a say in the pregnancy."

"Have you forgotten who has to carry these cubs?"

"Izzie, you're not honestly worried about being pregnant? I don't care how much weight you gain as long as you and the cubs are healthy."

She sighed. "You honestly think I'm concerned about gaining weight? How could you even think that? You know why I'm not fit to be a mother."

"How could you suggest killing our cubs?" In a much calmer voice, he said, "You know what children mean to me and my family."

Years ago, my son met up with a witch. Things didn't end well between them, and she cursed the James family. My grandson was an only child. The love of a true mate broke the spell. Izzie's pregnancy was a blessing.

"I-I'm sorry. I forgot." Izzie's voice cracked. "Hunter, forgive me?"

It was time for me to speak before my grandchildren made an irreversible decision.

I knocked and asked, "Can I come in?"

The lock disengaged, and the door opened. "What is it, Baba? Izzie and I are—"

Silently, I placed my arms around them. "I love the both of you. We are family, and we'll get through this time."

Izzie said, "But, Baba, I don't think I can do this."

I stepped back and put my hand on her slightly rounded stomach. "Don't think. Feel. There is life inside you, granddaughter. Those cubs are a blessing to you and Hunter."

"That's what I tried to tell her, Baba."

"Well, you were doing a poor job. For starters, never argue with a pregnant female. It unleashes bad vibes. We need happiness in this house." I removed my hand.

My granddaughter crossed her arms. "Perhaps you should tell my mother."

"I'll speak with Arleta. In the meantime, no more rash decisions. See the doctor. Make sure the babes are healthy." My gaze bounced from Izzie to Hunter. "Understood?"

"Yes, Baba. We'll call Dr. Underwood right now," said Hunter.

Izzie's eyebrows pulled together, the crease between them deepening. The stress she was putting on herself wouldn't be good for the young. For their sake, I prayed she'd change her thinking.

Although Dr. Underwood gave Izzie a clean bill of health yesterday, my granddaughter was still troubled. Originally, I thought her melancholy was about not knowing the number of young she carried. I realized how distressing that could be. When my daughter-in-law had been pregnant with Hunter, she prayed she'd give birth to three or four cubs. Her agony, however, was about the family curse.

And Izzie's?

As the day wore on, I realized something else was behind her anguish. I couldn't help but think back to that peculiar feeling I had the morning my grandchildren shared the news. The curious impression hadn't abated. It only became stronger with each passing day.

Could it explain Izzie's gloom and doom?

I found my grandson staring into a raging fire, his laptop beside him on the sofa. With the snow falling and the lights twinkling on our tree, it could have been a perfect scene. His woebegone expression, however, spoiled the mood.

"What's wrong, *noxhuiutze*?"

My use of the ancient language made him look up. "Oh, hey, Baba."

I sat on a nearby chair. "Talk to me."

Hunter dragged a hand through his hair. "Honestly? I'm concerned about how many cubs we might be expecting. We're going to need a bigger house."

I chuckled.

"What's so funny?"

"There's plenty of time before you face that problem. When they arrive, all my great-grandchildren will need is one room. Perhaps it's time for you to give up your private space downstairs."

If remodeled, it could be turned into a suite for Arleta.

My grandson's eyes bulged. "You know about that?"

"I'm old, not stupid. I've known about your sexual activity for far too long. Thing is, you have always been a healthy male with normal needs. Your actions weren't for me to judge." I leaned back and crossed my legs at the ankles. "So tell me the real problem. What's truly bothering you?"

"Izzie."

Of course.

He shook his head. "I don't understand. She hasn't shown one ounce of happiness about the pregnancy. When she took the test, Izzie cried. I thought somebody had died."

"Did you think a visit with the doctor would change her mood?"

Hunter's mouth slackened briefly, and he scratched his jaw. "I was hoping it would. I figured once the shock wore off, she'd be excited. Baba, I'd do anything to make this easier for her."

My grandson had a good heart. He wanted the best for the female he loved more than life. So did I.

Family was important to Naguals. Our people had always believed in a sound foundation comprised of mates with their cubs surrounding them. Living in a household with grandparents, aunts, uncles, and lots of cousins was a blessing. Over time, Nagual clans became smaller until they were a rarity. If I wanted the tradition to continue, we had to do our part.

I have to help my grandchildren, or I might never see another generation thrive.

"Maybe I can help Izzie," I said.

Hunter blew air through his cheeks and shut down his computer. "Sorry, Baba. I think it might take a miracle to change Izzie's mind."

Glancing over at Hunter, I said, "Sometimes miracles exist in simple things."

My grandson's voice cracked as he continued, "Even after seeing Dr. Underwood, she still wants to terminate the cubs."

I won't let that happen.

"What do you want, *noxhuiutze?*"

Hunter's answer was important. He couldn't be unsure about fatherhood. He needed my help, too. No half measures from me.

He scrubbed a hand over his face. Hunter looked at me and appeared much older. Somehow, the question had aged the male.

"I want a family with Izzie. Healthy cubs I can share our history and the stories you told me. I thought—" Hunter cleared his throat. "I thought Izzie wanted the same thing. Am I asking too much?"

"No. You only have to ask the spirits."

My grandson rolled his eyes. He realized the Supreme One created all life, but Hunter wasn't spiritual. Even as a cub, he shied away from the rituals I performed. With adolescence came more doubt. Eventually, I gave up trying to teach him all of our ways. I assumed one day he'd make the journey on his own and discover enlightenment.

"Although it's not your way, I'll implore the spirits."

Hunter lifted his laptop and pushed to his feet. "See if those spirits can talk some sense into my wife before it's too late."

Oh, the spirits had something to say. I was sure of it.

Honoring my promise to Izzie had to be my first action. Although I would have liked to avoid it, I had to speak with Arleta. Maybe the female didn't realize how her words hurt Izzie.

When I arrived at her room, Arleta's door was open. She sat on the bed, knitting what appeared to be a tiny blanket for the cubs. My old heart filled with joy seeing her engaged in something positive.

I knocked, and she looked up. "Can we talk?"

"Of course, Baba. Come in."

Arleta, not the tidiest houseguest, had piled the only available seat with discarded clothing. After closing it, I leaned against the door.

"What's on your mind?"

"I'm concerned about Izzie. She's so against being a mother she wants to end the pregnancy."

Arleta gasped and put down her project. "I'll go talk to her right—"

"I don't think that's a good idea."

The female pursed her lips, then after a moment, she said, "You think I'm responsible."

"Tell me I'm wrong. Tell me what you think is troubling your daughter."

She sighed. "Maybe you should have asked Izzie. I told her—"

"Tell *me*. Help me understand, so I can help her."

"Fine. Did you know her father left me? It came out of the blue. One day he was there, and the next he wasn't. I tried making ends meet. My mother even moved in with us to help. But without my mate, I was dying inside."

"So you went to find him?"

"Yes, but catching up with him wasn't easy. I tracked him to Spain but then the trail ran cold. Eventually, I found him when he moved to Colorado. Then I learned the bastard replaced me and the kids. New wife. New family. I was an idiot."

"Why didn't you return to your children?"

"Embarrassment. How could I have faced my mother's ridicule or theirs?" Arleta paused briefly. "I thought Izzie forgave me."

"So did I."

"This is what's stressing her out?" Arleta shook her head. "She needs to get over it. Pregnancy is difficult for the females in my family. Every time I was pregnant, I lost a cub or two. Baba, worrying too much could kill Izzie."

I always suspected anxiety could be bad for the babies. Truthfully, I hadn't considered what it might do to my granddaughter.

Thinking there might be some type of herb or oil to help Izzie, I put on my hat and coat and left the house. Hunter had offered to drive me to Town Square—it was a considerable walk from Creekwood Estates—but I needed the exercise despite the chill in the air. Besides, the distance would allow me to ponder the situation while appreciating the festive decorations. Normally, I enjoyed the bright lights along with the glitter and glitz of the holidays. If it hadn't been for the dismal state my granddaughter was in, I would have gone for a walk just to sightsee.

Izzie's distress wasn't affecting only her. Hunter was troubled, too. Since meeting Izzie, he'd changed. Although he hadn't given up his membership with the Swords of the Infernal Night motorcycle club or stopped working for Brian Long, the accountant, my grandson kept better hours now. He no longer frequented the Haven Saloon either. When I asked Hunter, he said he disliked spending too much time away from Izzie. Her stress, however, might have him repeating bad habits. Something I didn't want for him.

Thinking I might find some sort of beneficial elixir, I entered Howe's Herbal Shoppe. Ruby's granddaughter was very helpful, showing me the vast assortment of vitamins along with herbs and oils, but nothing seemed like the right thing to ease Izzie's distress. Young Scarlet wished me a good day as I left the shop.

A preoccupied mind and walking never mixed nicely. Next thing I knew, I collided with someone. "Oof!"

I glanced up. "Oh, I'm so sorry, Courtney."

The silver-haired, petite female shifter smiled. "Is everything all right, Baba? I've never known you to walk around in a fog."

I chuckled. "There's a lot on my mind."

She dipped her chin. "The holidays are difficult for everyone. So much going on in our lives. Can I help you with anything? Maybe just lend an ear?"

With gifts to buy, homes to decorate, and meals to prepare... It could be overwhelming. Maybe talking about my concerns would help.

Courtney, part of the McCabe mountain lion pride, could answer a question for me. "Do you know anything about females pregnant with multiple young?"

She laughed. "Have you forgotten I was a nurse and that I'm a twin? Tell me what's going on."

"Hunter and Izzie are expecting."

"Congratulations!" Her joy evaporated like summer rain. "It is good news, right?"

"It should be." I stepped to the side as someone walked

toward the shop door. "But I'm concerned about Izzie's welfare. Her mother said pregnancy was difficult for the females in the Itzae family."

Courtney nodded. "Of course, I don't know the details of her case since I'm no longer practicing. It is well-documented, though, that females carrying multiple babes can have special health needs. Any stress jeopardizes the viability of the babies."

Precisely my concern.

The female touched my shoulder. "My advice?"

"Please."

"Izzie should follow Dr. Underwood's instructions closely. If something feels weird to her, she should let him know."

Who should I contact when things felt off to me?

As I stood there speaking with Courtney, I felt a growing unease. After I thanked her, I walked away, but the feeling didn't dissipate.

Maybe I was wrong to think Arleta contributed to her daughter's distress. It was quite possible the anxiety lingering in the air triggered Izzie's apprehension. The thought stayed with me as I walked through the snow-covered streets bedecked with tinsel, lights, and other festive decorations. Everywhere I went, that general weirdness followed me.

Before I knew it, I was standing on the sidewalk outside of Broastful Brew. As soon as I pushed open the door, Sunny Blackstone waved. The young lady recently graduated from the Sun and Moon Academy high school and was filling in for Macy. Right as I was about to order my usual cup of coffee with a bit of chicory, I glimpsed Ikal Tayute.

I told Sunny she could help the next customer and went over to Ikal's table. "Hello, my friend."

He gave me a forlorn grin and then looked down at his cup of tea.

I almost asked what troubled him, but deep down, I knew. Last year, Ikal lost his beloved wife. She hadn't been sick. It was just her time. Sitting across from him, I placed my hands on the table.

"I hadn't expected to see you here today, Baba."

We met regularly on Fridays to have coffee and exchange ideas. It was Monday. "I've a lot on my mind."

"The strangeness in the air?" asked Ikal.

I flinched slightly. "Yes. You feel it, too?"

My friend nodded. "Honestly, I thought it was the season changing. Then, I thought about Zuma. You know, she loved the holidays. I figured it was simply my missing her creating the weird feeling."

"Mr. Chapula?" It was Sunny. The girl's disposition matched her name. In her hand was my cup of coffee. "I thought I'd bring this over."

"Thank you, dear. I so appreciate it."

"You're welcome." She smiled brightly and then headed back to the counter.

I added a splash of cream. As I stirred the mixture, I watched Ikal. I was thankful he was close to his grandson. Although Monte was building a life with his soul mate in their home, the young male insisted Ikal move in with them.

Ikal cleared his throat. "You should come over soon. Pandora's cooking has improved."

I chuckled. "Good to hear. Can she make fry bread yet?"

"She's learning. Maybe she'll perfect it by Christmas."

Ah, the holidays were upon us, but nobody would enjoy them until I found a way to make things right.

Speaking with Ikal helped clarify some things. The town was in desperate need of something. What exactly? I couldn't be sure.

My problem was twofold. First, I needed to narrow down what ailed the residents of Havenwood Falls. Then, I had to acquire the proper tools to accomplish the job.

The similarity between Ikal's and Izzie's sadness stood out. Izzie hadn't experienced the same type of loss my friend did, but they both suffered from a pervasive melancholy. I felt it from others while walking through the streets, as though the whole town had a shared case of anxiety.

During the holidays, plenty of people became overwhelmed. When Hunter was a cub, his mother would drive herself crazy preparing for the festivities. To ease her spirit, I would perform a peace ceremony for the family. But that was an intimate gathering for a handful of people. I needed something for a large crowd. Blessing an entire town was a gigantic undertaking.

An object with inherent power might help, but the magic had to be specific. I planned to heal everyone in Havenwood Falls and the town we lived in.

By the time I reached Madame Tahini's and Master Wu's Potions, Lotions, Palm Readings and Other Extra-Sensory Services, I had a plan. Hopefully, Madame Tahini could help bring it to fruition.

The shop was owned by a female fae named Teeny Weeny and now with her new husband, Tang Wu. Unlike her, nothing was small about her business. Everything about her salon—from the built-in redwood bookcases filled with colorful books and the enormous chair at a round table—seemed best suited for much larger individuals. The minute peephole, placed low on the door, was the only clue someone within those walls might be height challenged.

I followed the slender being through the dark foyer and stopped before the claw-footed table. She glanced up at me. "Baba, I've been expecting you. What can I do for you today?"

"Where should I begin?" I mumbled.

Teeny Weeny frowned. "I sense there's something troubling your heart."

"There is. Hunter and Izzie are expecting. My granddaughter is less than happy about the blessed event. Hunter could use some uplifting, too." I sighed. "Even my friend Ikal seems so sad. It's like…" My words trailed off. Just talking about everyone's sorrow made my heart ache a little.

Teeny Weeny bobbed her head. "You speak about the strange sensations traveling through the town. Something tells me you've already come up with a solution."

"I have. What do you think of the odd feelings?"

"They trouble me. The feeling is like a tremor under the terrain."

I'd been thinking more along the lines of a disturbance in the atmosphere. If Teeny Weeny felt it beneath the Earth and I felt it in the air, then my assumption about it being pervasive was accurate.

"I believe Havenwood Falls needs an infusion of peace. Although I'm a shaman, I've never attempted to blanket an entire town before."

The tiny shop owner tapped her chin and then held up a finger. "I have just what you need to propagate peace throughout our beautiful burg."

She went over to a cupboard and pulled out a wooden box. Lifting the lid, Teeny Weeny removed a black velvet bag. She brought it to me and then opened it. Inside was a mess of blue-green round stones.

I held one in my hand. Immediately, a surge of calm passed through me. Looking down, I asked, "What is this?"

"A stone called amazonite. The crystal supports healing and harmony. Just holding one instills balance and good feelings."

Agreed. But would the stone be enough?

"Do you think it would be appropriate for a peace ceremony?"

Teeny Weeny's eyes brightened. "Yes, I do. Everyone in town would benefit without need of any type of potion."

We needed an easy way for everyone to have the stones. "Perhaps we could distribute a piece of amazonite to as many people as possible. But is carrying such a tiny thing in a pocket enough? It could be easily lost that way."

"I have plenty of these, thanks to my pixie girls who have found a new obsession in collecting them, and they're all drilled to be strung. If everyone bears the beads as a bracelet, that might accomplish your goal."

"A perfect idea!"

Teeny Weeny and I spent the next half hour collecting all the amazonite beads she had stuffed away in her drawers and cabinets. Once gathered, I sanctified the objects with a prayer. A little extra magic never hurt.

Designing the bracelet was easy. Thankfully, Teeny Weeny had plenty of stretchable elastic for the purpose.

Although Hunter might question the expense, I was certain he'd understand after I explained the situation to him. I placed my wallet in my pocket and lifted my box of supplies.

Teeny Weeny walked with me to the door. "I'll make sure shop owners and those outside of town get a handful to distribute to their customers. I think this will be fabulous fun!"

"I do, too."

As I left Madame Tahini's, I reached for my phone and called Hunter. The box was heavy, and I didn't relish the idea of lugging it up the hill to his house.

He answered on the first ring. "Hi, Baba."

"Can you pick me up? I'm in front of Madame Tahini's."

"Sure thing. I'm just down the street. See you in a couple of minutes."

I sighed and smiled to myself. Teeny Weeny and I had a means to instilling peace. Now, I had to find a way to spread the word throughout Havenwood Falls.

❄

When Hunter pulled up to the curb, he eyed the big box in my arms. After he took it from me, we got into the SUV.

"What's in the package, Baba?"

"A plan. But I'll tell you more when we get home. I'd like to tell you and Arleta at the same time."

Hunter nodded. "All right."

I hoped they would be as enthusiastic about the project as I was. Thankfully, it took a shorter time reaching Creekwood Estates than my trip away from it.

After we arrived, Hunter went to find Arleta. It didn't take long before the pair walked into the great room and sat near the fireplace.

"Okay, Baba. What's this about?" Hunter asked.

"I think whatever's bothering Izzie is spreading through town."

His eyes widened. "What? An illness?"

"No. Nothing like that. There's a lot of anxiety. The holidays tend to worry people for many reasons. Sometimes it's the death of a loved one."

"Like Monte's grandmother?"

"Right. Sometimes it's being separated from our families. Whatever the cause, that sentiment is right here in Havenwood Falls. I think a peace ceremony would help."

Arleta tilted her head. "When I was a cub, I heard of them. Do they really work?"

"If done correctly, and as long as everyone is welcome." I tapped the box. "What's inside will help."

Hunter jerked his chin toward it. "What's in there?"

I opened the container and removed a handful of gems. "This is amazonite. Just hold it in your hands and tell me what you think." I gave one each to my grandson and his mother-in-law.

Arleta sighed while Hunter grinned.

"Baba, how is this possible?" he asked. "Suddenly, I don't have any worries."

"Keep that one on you." I closed the lid. "I want to conduct a peace ceremony for the entire town. We'll call it the Magic of Peace Ceremony."

Hunter gazed up at the ceiling briefly and then said, "The best spot would be Town Square Park. Mayor Barbie should definitely be there. So should Saundra Beaumont."

Arleta added, "How about the preacher from the town church? He might help the non-magical feel more comfortable in participating."

Realizing the number of bracelets we had to distribute, I said, "Maybe we can get Luna Coven members or some students from the Sun and Moon Academy to help us."

"When do you want to have the ceremony?" Hunter asked.

"As soon as possible. In the next few days," I said.

My grandson shook his head. "Baba, we could use a week, maybe two, to organize everything."

"No," I insisted, my voice rising. "Waiting isn't an option. Much is at stake."

Hunter blew air through his cheeks. "All right, Baba. We'll get it done, but people need more than a few days. Even if SIN helps spread the word, the weekend would be best, and if it's on Saturday, it can be before the Hot Cocoa and Cookie Crawl. We stand a better chance of having a large turnout if people have more than a couple of days' notice."

Understood.

As soon as Hunter departed, Arleta sat beside the box and peered into it. "How will you turn loose stones into wearables?"

Although my fingers weren't arthritic, I couldn't craft hundreds of bracelets this fast. What was I thinking?

Arleta touched my wrist. "Hey, you have me. Maybe we can get Izzie to help."

"This project requires more than three people."

"I'm willing to stay up all night if needed." Suddenly, Arleta's face brightened. "I might be able to get some others to give us a hand. You mentioned those students. I bet if we told them what we're doing, they'd offer to make the bracelets."

"Actually, that's an excellent idea. This is an all-inclusive event we're planning. Making the bracelets should be as well. I'll go—"

"Nonsense." Arleta rose from the sofa. "Allow me to go out and talk to people. You've done so much already."

With all the walking I'd done, I felt a bit tired. "Thank you. I think I'll rest a bit before making dinner."

She shook her head. "You'll do no such thing."

"Oh?"

"Put up your feet and relax. I'll pick up something for dinner while I'm out." Arleta reached into the box, pulled out a handful of crystals and string, and placed the items in my lap. "If you get bored, work on the design while I'm gone. When I return with our helpers, I'll make hot cocoa for everyone."

"Thank you, Arleta."

"You are so welcome, Baba." The female headed toward the front door.

Despite Izzie's feelings about her mother, Arleta's heart was in a better place. She had good intentions for her daughter and grandchildren. I also believed she had noble wishes for Havenwood Falls.

Arleta and the students from the Sun and Moon Academy finished the bracelets in record time. To make the bracelets even more beneficial, at one of the witch's recommendations, we made them with twenty-seven beads each, which allowed it to be used as a pocket mala. Four times around would equal the 108 beads on a full-size mala, one for each energy center in the body. They could also be used as prayer beads. Integrating the diversity that was Havenwood Falls made them even more perfect.

Hunter and the motorcycle club spread the word around town, too. Everything—and everyone—was ready for the ceremony this evening.

Well, *almost* everyone.

Izzie had spent the last two days in the bedroom she shared with Hunter. He tried to talk to her, but she wouldn't speak to him either. The situation became so dire, he stopped sleeping in their room.

At one point, he came to me and asked about the amazonite.

"Baba, do you think we could place the stones inside her totem?" he'd asked.

I considered it for a moment and then said, "Provided Izzie will remove it. Yes, I think I could do that."

My granddaughter, however, refused to take off the talisman. Enough was enough. If she continued sulking, she'd lose the cubs. Despite her reluctance to be a mother, I didn't think she could endure the agony that came with losing young.

I knocked on the door. When no one answered, I turned the knob and entered the room. Izzie hadn't turned on any lights. I reached for the lamp and then wished I hadn't.

My poor, sweet granddaughter huddled in a corner with a knitted blanket around her shoulders. Tears stained her cheeks, and her hair needed a good brushing.

"Izzie…" I walked over and tried to help her up, but she pushed me away.

"Leave me be."

"No. I can't do that." I reached into my pocket and removed a bracelet. When I attempted to put in on her wrist, she shrieked and pulled away. But in her condition, I was stronger and refused to give up.

The change in her demeanor was almost instantaneous. Her face brightened, and her eyes seemed clearer when she looked at me.

"What did you do?"

I patted her hand. "What needed to be done. You mean the world to me, *ixhuiuhcihuapilli.*"

"Granddaughter?"

I nodded.

"You never called me that before."

"And I'm sorry. I should have said it the day you married Hunter."

Honestly, I had no excuse for my failure. Part of me assumed Izzie knew how I felt, but I was wrong. People had to hear our hearts. Our families and friends had to know, without a shadow of doubt, they were special.

"If the Great One deems it, I want to be a part of my great-grandchildren's lives."

She shook her head. "But, Baba, I'm not fit to be a mother."

"Do you want to be one?"

Her hands rested on her stomach. "I-I think so."

I wrapped my arms around Izzie's shoulders. "Nobody comes into this world ready to be a parent. We all must learn the way. That's why we have family and communities like Havenwood Falls. It really takes a village to raise children."

Suddenly, she hugged me. "Thank you, Baba."

"You're welcome." Sitting back, I said, "Now, it's time for us to get ready. The entire family must be a part of the ceremony. We can't do this without you."

An hour later, the residents of Havenwood Falls and many tourists gathered in town square. As requested, someone laid and lit a bonfire. Although residents could pick up a bracelet at the different shops over the past few days, Arleta brought extras along with candles. Volunteers distributed the items to anyone who didn't have them.

A tall woman with puffy blonde hair streaked with red and green approached us. Beside her was a female with silvery-white hair twisted up on her head.

I smiled. "Mayor Barbie. Saundra. Thank you for allowing me to do this."

The mayor grinned. "I'm glad you thought of it. The air has seemed off lately. I thought it was the weather."

"I'll admit to having the same thought," said the Beaumont witch. "Did you need help with anything else, Baba?"

My gaze went to the altar, facing the bonfire. Pine boughs and poinsettia decorated the surface, including an unexpected cat figurine carved from amazonite.

"Cece asked if we could include it," Saundra said. "I didn't think it was a problem."

I shook my head. "It is fine. I think we're ready to start. If everyone has their bracelets and candles…"

Mayor Barbie said, "I'll get their attention." The woman headed for a microphone and said, "Ladies and gentlemen, boys and girls, we're ready to start the ceremony."

Arleta grasped my elbow. "We've got this, Baba."

She was right. I was a shaman. It didn't matter the size of the crowd. Only the size of their hearts. Right on cue, Pastor Leandros, a human preacher, walked over with the mayor and Saundra.

"Mayor Barbie, you'll do the welcome and introduce everyone. Saundra, you should say a few words, too." Looking toward the preacher, I added, "If you wouldn't mind doing the closing?"

"That would be my honor," he said, giving me a cheesy smile.

While the mayor welcomed everyone, I checked out the arrangement on top of the altar. Everything was there—a larger amazonite gem, white candles, a set of oracle cards, a pot of specially brewed tea, a wooden bowl of water, a jar of soil, and incense. The items represented peace and four of the five elements—fire, water, earth, and air. Someone included a gold lighter. The park served as the fifth element —space.

Saundra stepped up to the microphone. "We all seem to be struggling with finding peace a little more than usual this year. We have Baba Chapula to thank for recognizing the need for this evening's ceremony and bringing it all together. We also send our gratitude to Madame Tahini for providing the amazonite crystals everyone is wearing. Amazonite is a stone that supports balance, harmony, and peace within, exactly what so many of us seem to need right now. If you don't have a bracelet or candle, raise your hand, and one of our volunteers will bring you one."

Saundra finished speaking, and we waited until the last of the bracelets and candles were distributed. Then the ceremony began.

"We start with the lighting of the candle. As Arleta comes around, each person is to light their individual candle from the larger one. This simple act unites us as a community," I said.

Izzie's mother lit a large white candle and then walked over to a resident. It took a few minutes before everyone held their own lit candle.

I turned to Saundra. "Could you help me, please?"

"Of course. What do you need?"

"If you wouldn't mind pouring the tea." I looked around but didn't see what I needed.

"Missing something?"

"There should be a gold goblet."

Saundra smiled and pointed to the altar. "Look beneath it."

Sure enough. The item was tucked into a corner. *How strange.* I thought I looked there.

Winking at me, the witch poured the tea.

I lifted the cup and said, "May peace exist on Earth and in Havenwood Falls. May everyone show love for one another, too."

Instead of passing around the goblet, I took a sip while Arleta lit the incense. She handed it to me, and I waved it over my head three times, clockwise. "May our fears and worries be carried to the stars. Only positivity will rain down upon us."

I inserted the incense into the container of soil.

My next words were for the ancients, the Great One, and anyone who knew the Nahuatl language. Roughly translated, the words meant:

> Oh, Great One and sacred Ancestors,
> Teach us love, compassion, and honor
> Heal our town and heal all of us
> Let us know peace.
> As long as the moon rises,
> The rivers flow,
> The sun shines,
> And the grasses grow,
> Let us know peace.

As I chanted the words, I raised my hands and performed the steps only known to me.

Arleta said to the crowd, "We asked everyone to write their fears, concerns, or the names of loved ones on a slip of paper. Now step toward the bonfire and release those papers."

It was a symbolic letting go, necessary to put the past where it belonged. Once everyone had done so, they received a clean slate from our great maker.

"Oh, Great Spirit, we lift our hands to you, the elements, and the Great Mother," I said. "Guide us and teach us to love one another. To respect one another. To be kind to one another, so we may live in peace."

Saundra came to the microphone again. I removed my drum from beneath the altar and began the rhythmic beating in the background as she spoke. "We'll now have a few moments of silence to connect with the peace spreading around us. Your bracelets have the right number of beads to serve as a pocket mala, if you'd like to repeat for each one the mantra of 'Shanti' or simply the word 'peace' to add another layer to the energy we're raising tonight. Feel it as its power weaves through the streets and settles over our town. Look inside yourselves and envision what peace means to you. Let the feeling stretch outward and upward. Lift this glorious energy to the heavens, so it may rain down upon us."

I beat my drum harder and louder, the sound representing the Earth's own heartbeat. As the energy from our thoughts continued to rise, the pace and volume of my drumming increased. Seeing the uplifted faces let me know I was doing a good thing… Correction. *We* were doing a good thing for Havenwood Falls.

When the beating had been completed, I said, "Let us turn to each other in peace."

If anyone asked me, that was the best part of the ceremony. Residents hugged and shook hands. I overheard individuals say how they felt so much better.

As the goodwill moment ended, I nodded first toward Saundra.

The witch moved to the microphone and said, "Blessed be the beautiful energy and peace that have gone out this evening. May each of you continue to bask in its glow from this night forward. Use your bracelet as a reminder of this evening and to lift the energy of peace whenever you feel so called."

She gestured to Pastor Leandros, who traded places with her. He cleared his throat and said, "May tonight be a return to peace within. May you trust your highest power. You're exactly who you should be at this moment. May faith carry you as you recall all the infinite things you can do. Use your gifts and spread love. And the congregation said, Amen."

The crowd replied, "Amen."

I thanked the man for his benediction and then said, "Our ceremony has concluded. Remember you can find solitude in one another. A simple phone call or a shared cup of tea can be the inspiration to talk. When we tell each other our concerns, they're not so overwhelming."

After the ceremony ended, residents lingered around the bonfire. Near the altar, an interesting exchange happened between Izzie and Arleta. I couldn't hear the words, but I noticed the older female smiling right before she hugged her daughter.

Hunter walked up to me and clapped my shoulder. "You did good, Baba. This was exactly what we all needed."

I grinned.

Nothing could ever beat the magic of peace.

Merry Christmas from the James/Itzae/Chapula family!

Have you read Hunter and Izzie's story by Nadirah Foxx?
  Taming the Beast

REBORN

BY MORGAN WYLIE

A Blackstone Witch Hunters Christmas Story

*H*avenwood Falls in the winter had to be the most beautiful place. The town went all-out with decorations and festivities. The town square was lavished with lights, garland, poinsettias, and piped-in Christmas music. All the businesses around the square participated in the decor. Excitement ensued with anticipated events such as the annual Hot Cocoa and Cookie Crawl, the Cold Moon Ball, and the New Year's Eve torch parade and fireworks. But this year something new would transpire. This year, the town would come together for a special candle-lighting ceremony put on by the James-Itzae family called the Magic of Peace. Many of the businesses would supply the town's people with a special gemstone called amazonite said to offer peace and healing to those who need it.

"So, Brock, let's go over the plans for the upcoming events. With the last-minute addition of the peace ceremony, there is a lot going on," Reggie Blackstone, Brock's father and head of the Blackstone family businesses, initiated. Brock, his father Reggie, and Brock's younger brother Brice met together in the front windows of the currently closed Soothing Sips winetasting room set on the east side of the town square.

"I know as a front on the square especially, and maybe even at the winery, we'll be participating in handing out bracelets for the peace ceremony and cookies and cocoa at the Cookie Crawl in a few days, correct?" Brock asked, looking down at his calendar. Brock was always organized and thought through everything several steps before he even needed to.

"Yes, and your mom, Aunt Letti, Hollis, and Macy, if she has time, are concocting what they've deemed to be 'The Best Blackstone Cocoa Ever' to enter the contest along with great-great-grandma Marie Blackstone's cookies to share during the Cookie Crawl." Reggie shook his head with a small smile. "They've never won, but they keep trying."

Brice and Brock laughed.

"Well, at least they keep trying. Maybe Sunny could help them out this year. She might be able to add in something different. Who knows? I'll ask her," Brice said, excited at his new revelation.

"Sounds good. Luckily, because of the Cookie Crawl, we were already staffed to handle the extra crowd who might overflow from the ceremony. Brice, are you able to help at Soothing Sips during the crawl? Oh wait, you're still not of age," Brock said with forgetful sarcasm. "Could you hurry up and turn twenty-one already?" Brock slugged his brother playfully in the arm.

"Ouch, watch it! Could you hurry up and find a girl already?" Brice chided, equally playfully though the words stung Brock.

A moment of silence then Brice apologized. "Sorry, man. I didn't mean that. I was just retaliating."

"All good, little brother. And I know you'll get legal one of these days. I just can't wait for us to expand our empire, but I need you fully in the partnership wheel for us to do that. I don't really have time for a girl right now, nor have I found one that sticks yet. Plus, we have the launch of our new *Holiday House* brew the night of the crawl as well!"

The brothers fist bumped, and all was fine.

"Brock, did you plan to attend the Cold Moon Ball this year? If so, I can find someone else to man that event the following weekend," his father prodded.

A brief moment of uncertainty passed over his face then Brock shook his head. "Not this year, Dad. I'm all yours. I thought about asking one of the girls who frequent the winery, but I'm not really feeling it."

"What about Chalise? I've seen you eye her. She seems cool," Brice offered nonchalantly even though the small smirk he tried to hide belied his casual nature.

Brock's eyes shot to Brice. "Nah, she's…she's cool and all, but I don't think we'd have anything in common."

"Why not? I mean she's already connected to our family in a way, since she's from Ryne's family phoenix clan. She's been here for a little while now, what six months?"

"Eight," Brock corrected, unaware of the look that passed between Brice and his father.

"Right, so all I'm saying is it might be worth starting a convo with her. That's it," Brice concluded.

"She's come over to the house a couple times with Hollis and Ryne and seems like she's very nice. I will add—as your father—that she comes from an intense background. The phoenix clan Ryne's grandfather is chief of does not conduct business the way we would, son. She may have some baggage to work through still as she adjusts to the freedom of our lives in Havenwood Falls."

"We all have baggage of some sort, Dad," Brock mumbled then slapped his knee and sat up straight. "If the opportunity comes up, perhaps I'll talk to her, but today we have business to finish."

"All right, boys, back on track," Reggie agreed. "Also, you can display more of your microbrews in the window whenever you're ready. Make sure the display adds to the festive arrangements of the other windows but feel free to have fun with it. And I think that's all we had on the agenda today," Reggie concluded their meeting. "Have a good day, boys!"

"You too, Dad," they both said.

They stood up and went their individual ways. But Brock couldn't help but spot the fiery redhead, Chalise, out the window, walking along the path through the square with two of her friends. As if his thoughts called out to her, she turned toward Soothing Sips, her eyes locking momentarily onto Brock's gaze. Then Chalise turned back to her friends with a smile on her face as if nothing had transpired.

But something had expanded in his chest. Something he had never felt before. Something he wasn't sure he could live up to.

"Hey, Brock, how's it going?" Ryne asked as he, Gallad, and Macy walked into the Stone Falls Winery. The weather had snowed on and off for days, and even though it was light, it had been piling up outside. But inside, the fire crackled and the holiday lights glowed. Music played softly in the background; not too loud so the patrons couldn't talk over it, but just enough to add to the atmosphere—it was almost magical. Ryne Calloway, half witch and half phoenix, was not often seen without Hollis Blackstone on his arm. Gallad Augustine and Macy Blackstone, who had prolonged their engagement until after they graduated from the supernatural college, hadn't had a lot of free time lately with classes and work, but with the holidays looming, they seemed to be out and about. To Brock, they were a welcome sight.

"Not bad, not bad. What brings you three in today? You're

not scheduled to work at the inn today are you, Sprite?" Brock's nickname for his sister brought an endearing smile to her face.

"Nope, we needed a break from studying for finals, so we're out doing a little Christmas shopping," Macy replied, pulling off her red and pink plaid scarf, shaking the snow off her already white-blonde hair while they saddled themselves up to the bar top.

"I needed a little help with what to get Hollis this year," Ryne admitted, taking off his jacket, "so I enlisted your sister."

"She's a good shopper. I'm sure you'll find something. Can I get you all something to drink?" Brock wiped down the counter next to them where a small group had just finished and left.

"We want to try whatever micro you and Brice are working on," Gallad said with a sneaky smile, as he swiped back his dark hair away from his eyes. "I have it on good authority you may have a special holiday brew…brewing."

"You want to try it? We're keeping the tastings quiet until launch, but I know a guy who could hook you up." Excitement lit Brock's eyes as he described the rich flavor and smooth texture of his and Brice's newest creation. "It's a dark brew with a hint of pine—similar to last year—but we've added some holiday spices to it. I'm excited to release it officially at the crawl. It's already been out as a pre-order online, and so far the feedback has been encouraging."

"Sounds fantastic," Ryne said, mirroring the excitement Brock displayed. Gallad nodded his head in agreement.

"Macy, what will you—" The bell on the door dinged, and when Brock looked up, his words stalled. Walking into the winery was Chalise and three other girls Brock knew from town.

"Ladies, welcome. Please seat yourselves, and I'll be with you in a moment." Brock's throat was suddenly dry, and his hands shook.

"Brock? What was that about?" Macy whispered, nodding at his hand now holding a glass of water he'd pulled out from under the bar.

"Nothing, Mace." He cleared his throat and shook out his hand. "Now what did you want, Sprite? Your usual rosé?"

Macy's gaze bored deep into his own. Something in her look made him uneasy, and he broke her spell by reaching for glasses. Brock had never shared with anyone in his family how fully human he felt sometimes. He knew they loved him, and it didn't matter he was human. He knew he was good at what he did, and he was happy... mostly. But occasionally, the amount of "other" that surrounded him made him feel inferior. If he was honest, that was the reason he hadn't pursued Chalise as he would've another human or even a supe he knew he had no future with. Something about Chalise was different. Something about her had latched ahold of his soul, and he didn't think he could be who she needed him to be.

"Sure, Brock, sounds fine," Macy said, bringing him out of his thoughts. He didn't like the way Macy seemed to understand him more than he wanted her to. Macy turned to the side and took note of Chalise watching Brock out of the corner of her eye. Macy looked back at Brock with a suspicious expression on her face. "Go talk to her."

"Well, of course, I need to get all their orders once I get yours filled," Brock said, brushing off her meaning. Macy rolled her eyes.

Brock busied himself getting their drinks. "Let me know what you think of the micro, guys! I'll check back in a bit." Brock went over to the girls...women sitting at the coveted table in front of the fireplace.

"Welcome... Hi... Hello, ladies." He cleared his throat. "Excuse me. Have you had a chance to look over the menu? Can I answer any questions for you?" Brock realized if he didn't look at Chalise and simply pretended to only serve the others in the group, his nerves could relax. He'd never been nervous talking to girls in the past. Why was she different? He had to get over that. He took their orders, and when it came to Chalise, he didn't make eye contact, but she insisted on talking to him directly.

"Hi, Brock, what do you recommend? I like wine, but I also like beer. I heard a rumor that you have some great microbrews on tap and wondered what you think I should try?" Chalise knew his name. Her voice reached into the depths of his heart, the sound soothing and inviting at the same time. "Brock?" she prodded with confusion.

"You want to try one my microbrews?" He shook his head to snap out of whatever trance her voice put him in. Okay, his brews he could talk about. "I'd recommend our newest holiday release, called *Holiday House*. A couple of guys at the counter are trying it right now as well. I'm sure you could ask them what they think, or I could bring you a sample to try first."

"Not necessary. The name alone sounds amazing. I want to try it, please," Chalise said with a smile that lit fireworks in his chest. She had tied back her mane of red and gold curls, but it only made her blue eyes stand out more.

"I'll be right back with your order." Brock scurried away from their table and into the back room as seemingly professional as he could without it looking like he was running away to hide. In the back office, Brock sat and buried his head in his hands between his knees. He'd heard that could help lightheadedness, although he wasn't sure about stupidness.

"Brock?" Macy called out quietly as she stuck her head into the office doorway. "Brock, are you all right?"

Brock shook his head. "I don't know what's wrong with me. My tongue was tied. I couldn't even look her in the eyes, and her voice made me feel like a pre-pubescent boy. I wanted to melt into her lap and never get up. What the hell is that? I don't even know why I'm telling you this, Macy, sorry. I'm sure it's nothing."

"Nothing? Brock, don't you know what you're saying?"

Brock looked up into Macy's face, confused. He shook his head. "I can't even think straight. I don't know what you mean?"

"Well, I'm no expert, but I've heard of these types of things happening with some groups of supernaturals when they find their mates... soul mates... whatever. You get what I'm saying, right?"

Brock's face turned ashen. "I'm not a supernatural, Macy. That shouldn't be possible."

Macy shrugged. "You may not be an active hunter, Brock, but you still have the same blood that's in our family. Maybe a mating can still affect you even if you lean more toward the human side."

"No, it can't be me. Why would it be me? There are other guys more suited... more... just more." Brock began to pace in the small space. "She didn't choose this, right? Why would she want me? She wouldn't. She doesn't even know me. I'll just stay away. Then she can find someone else. That's what I'll do." Mind made up, Brock inhaled deeply and centered himself.

"I don't think it works that way, Brock. And why are you so hard on yourself? You're an amazing guy, and any girl, supernatural or not, should be lucky to be with you! And if she can't see that, then she doesn't deserve you."

"Thanks, Sprite, but I'm taking the option away from her." He kissed her on the top of her head, nodded to himself, then strolled out the door.

Back behind the bar, Brock quickly made up the drinks to be delivered to the ladies' table. Thankfully the other bartender had arrived for the next shift. Macy hugged her oldest friend as she went back to her seat at the bar and smiled as Ruby put on her apron, ready for work. "Ruby Jean, could you deliver these drinks to the table over by the fireplace, please?"

Ruby Jean Milton, a lynx shifter with strawberry-blonde hair, talked animatedly with her hands, which had caused a few spills and broken glasses, but the customers liked her. She and Macy had been best friends since kindergarten, and she was an excellent waitress. She had worked for Broastful Brew with Macy during high school and had been working for Stone Falls Winery the last year or so once she turned twenty-one.

Brock watched from the sidelines as Ruby delivered the drinks and saw the disappointment in Chalise's eyes when Ruby explained Brock was busy filling other drink orders. Ruby did a fantastic job, but he couldn't help but feel a pang of regret in his chest that he hadn't gotten to be close to Chalise once more. And when he overheard her mention his name to her friends and how she thought he was cute and had wished he would've come back so she could tell him how fantastic her drink had been, it made his heart happy. Macy flashed him a conspiratorial smile just before Chalise made her way to the bar and slipped him a piece of paper with her phone number on it, which he unfortunately had already decided not to call.

The Blackstones had been busy making preparations and handing out the amazonite beaded bracelets to those who had come into Soothing Sips looking for one. And as people came in, many stayed and tasted the various wines and special versions for those of the non-human variety. The tasting room was busy with more people converging on the town square than usual for this time of year. Brice handed out the bracelets, Macy and Sunny touched up decorations for the additional Christmas festivities, and his mom was in the secret weapons room beneath the store, taking inventory to ensure the weaponry was battle-ready should they be needed. They didn't expect anything, but when more folks from out of town showed up for the winter season skiing, sledding, etc., the members of the Court of the Sun and the Moon wanted to know they were ready to defend their town if need be. They couldn't help but recall how the Collector had attacked on Christmas Eve three years previous, and then again a year and a half ago. Since then it had been unnervingly quiet, but to be certain, this was as good of time as any.

"Hi, Brock!" Her voice—that voice that sent fireworks through his chest—sounded below the ladder he was currently on, fixing a fallen garland out front. Chalise.

"Hi." His mouth went dry, and he lost words. He closed his eyes and breathed in through his nose.

"Are you okay? I didn't mean to startle you."

And she was thoughtful too. He was a goner.

"Uh, yeah, I mean, yes, I'm fine, thanks." Brock climbed slowly down the ladder. "Did you come to get a bracelet for the Magic of Peace Ceremony? We still have quite a few inside the store."

"That would be great. I thought I had one already, but I couldn't find it." She laughed. "Leave it to me to get stressed out trying to find a bracelet to invoke peace."

Brock laughed with her, forgetting how nervous he'd been moments before. Then he made a mistake and looked into her eyes. He felt like he fell into deep pools of refreshing water, which then began to warm and turned to a haze of purple. When he pulled out of her trance, he noted her eyes were ringed with a fiery red, creating the purple hue. They both gasped as one and stepped back from each other. Chalise cocked her head and truly looked at Brock. He found no malice for who he was or that she had no choice in who her mate could be. That couldn't be right. Brock shook his head, turned away, and broke the moment. He wouldn't take her choice away. When he glanced back, he caught the expression on her face squish up into confusion. He didn't want to be the cause of that look.

"Uh…here. I'll get you a bracelet and be right back." Brock rubbed his hands down his face and ducked inside

Soothing Sips, ignoring the inquisitive looks on the members of his family's faces. He grabbed a bracelet and went back outside.

"Thanks, Brock." She held out her hand, standing in the middle of the sidewalk. Already people were setting up chairs across the street in the park and preparing the pits for the bonfire as it was an outside ceremony in the middle of winter. "Would you put it on for me?"

Brock looked down at her wrist then back at her face. "Oh…ah, okay." After their strange encounter, he was shocked she was even talking to him.

"It's such a beautiful mix of blue and green but mostly that shade of jade green is so intense," she commented. "I've always wanted a beaded mala and in the form of a bracelet is perfect, so I don't lose it."

He fumbled for a moment trying to figure out how to roll the bracelet onto her hand then paused. "A mala?"

"It's like prayer or rosary beads. The goal of it is to direct your thoughts and intentions." She paused, then added quietly under her breath, "We should talk about what happened just now."

His fingers brushed the soft flesh of her hand, and he couldn't help the tremor that shot through his own hand. He tried to roll the beads over her hand as quickly as he could. He had to change the subject. "Do you know much about the amazonite? From what I've read, it's mined somewhere near here. I don't know much, and I don't know if it really offers peace, but people believe it does."

"I believe it does too."

He felt her gaze intently on him; while he finished, she kept talking. He liked the sound of her voice.

"It's also commonly referred here in our state as Colorado Jade since it's more green than blue in this area. But it works best with intention, you know? Like how the James-Itzae family asked those attending to bring a piece of paper with whatever might be causing anxiety or pain written on it, and then I think we direct the energy of peace from the amazonite toward that anxiety. I've never done it, but it couldn't hurt to try it."

Finally finished with the bracelet, Brock stared at her for a moment. He had never heard her talk so much, and he was mesmerized by her.

She cleared her throat. "I know you don't know me well, Brock, but I'd like to get to know you. I feel this connection with you deep inside my soul." She placed her hand over her heart. "I think we should probably explore it... Would you like to attend the peace ceremony with me?" she asked. When she saw the look of shock on his face, she added, "Or, you know, we could maybe get a cup of coffee or something after."

"You're asking me? Why?" Brock stumbled back a step. His breath hitched, and his heart raced. "You're a phoenix... and I'm only... There are *other* types of people... better guys out there for you... I'm not... I shouldn't be..." He continued to back away, stumbling into the brick next to the door, feeling for the handle behind him.

"Brock? Brock, wait," she called after him.

"I have to go. You deserve better, Chalise." Brock turned and disappeared into the store behind him. He had never felt like such a coward or so uneasy in his own skin. If only he wasn't human, he might pursue the connection he felt with her.

Brock arrived early to set up Soothing Sips for the evening crowd. The ceremony wouldn't start until sunset, but once it was over and the Cookie Crawl began, Blackstone Brothers would officially launch their seasonal microbrew, *Holiday House*. In a way they'd not yet done, the Blackstones would be doing a simultaneous launch in both locations: Soothing Sips and the Stone Walls Winery in conjunction with their winter wine, *Enchantment*. Everything was ready, and Brock had over-staffed the night for the events. Both locations had been fully decorated in their holiday finest; the magic of the season was intoxicating to say the least.

Brock had spare time before the first event, so he put on his coat and hat and went out into the chill of the afternoon to help set up if he could. However, he didn't get far before a strange feeling stopped him in his tracks, almost forcing him to turn involuntarily in the opposite direction he had been heading. And who should be coming out of Coffee Haven but the one person he'd been trying to avoid—as much as was possible in a small town—but Chalise.

She looked like a beautiful winter angel wrapped in a white coat with white fur at the collar. Her bright red and gold hair tumbled down around her neck, accentuating her soft freckled face and bright blue eyes. As her eyes caught his, rings of red began to bleed into the blue, creating that same amazing purple hue. He knew her eyes could turn full red if she went more phoenix on him, but thankfully, since they were in full view of the town, she kept it tampered. Upon seeing him, she smiled, and her smile lit up his world. He wanted to run to her, the connection felt so strong and so natural, but he couldn't...wouldn't for her sake. Whether she knew it or not, she needed someone stronger.

Brock went against everything his instincts and his body told him to do and turned away from her. He couldn't help but look back one time, and when he saw the disappointment on her face, he wanted to comfort her. But he couldn't. Instead, he strode with purpose and pushed his legs to carry him away from town square. He drove around until he had nowhere else to drive and ended up at the winery to double-check their preparations for the evening launch.

Back on track. Business helped him focus.

Inside the winery, Ryne manned the bar and poured wine

for a couple. But Brock headed straight for the back office only to have Ryne close behind him. Brock had wanted to find peace and quiet, which he realized he wouldn't find at the winery. There were always at least a few people working or milling about.

"Hey, Brock, you okay man? You look a little shaken up," Ryne said and saddled up onto a stool at the edge of the office. The same rustic modern decor flowed from the public area out front throughout the back offices as well. Normally it provided a sense of comfort for Brock, but not today.

"I'll be fine, Ryne. We have a launch tonight," Brock said with a forced smile, trying to get himself back on track. He inhaled through his nose, inflating his chest, then slowly blew it out through his mouth. "How is everything here? Ready to go?"

Ryne paused for a moment and watched Brock, making him feel a little uncomfortable.

"You know we are. You were here late last night, and all is ready. It couldn't be more ready." Ryne folded his arms across his chest and took a step forward. They weren't done talking yet. "It's Chalise, isn't it? Ever since she came into town eight months ago, I've seen you watch her."

"Hey, man, I'm not starting anything with Chalise. I know she's like a sister to you."

Ryne held his hand out in front to stop Brock. "That's not what I mean. Yes, she's like a little sister to me. And when she escaped my grandfather's clan to find a better life for herself and tracked me down to come live here, I couldn't have been more proud of her. I want the very best for her. And I think that is you."

Brock was confused. "What do you mean? How could you think that? She's a phoenix and a powerful one at that, from what you've said of her abilities to transform back and forth so quickly and easily. She's so brave for leaving on her own and seeking a new way of life out. And I'm… I'm just…"

"What, Brock?"

"I'm just human," he vehemently spat out. "There I said it. I'm just human. I'm not strong enough for her. I'm not enough. I could never live up to who she deserves to be with. She deserves more."

"Damn straight she does. She deserves you to be all of you. Do you understand what I'm saying?"

Brock looked up at him, his expression defeated. He felt lost.

"I'm saying she deserves you to be you. Not to try and be someone else or who you *think* she needs you to be. You are a powerful and influential person in your own right, Brock Blackstone. And if she chooses you, then you are who she needs you to be."

"But that's just it," Brock interrupted. "She didn't choose me! Her mating mumbo jumbo did. I don't want her to be with me out of obligation or pity or anything other than desire. And if she isn't given that option, then I will take it away from her so she can choose someone else."

Ryne started laughing then stopped abruptly. "You don't know anything about our phoenix clan, do you? When a phoenix of our clan feels the mating pull, they are offered the choice of their mate. If they don't choose, then one can be provided for them by the phoenix powers that be. You should simply ask her about the connection you have because maybe it's her who isn't giving you much of a choice. Just something to think about. But I know here," he put his hand over his heart, "you could be someone special for her, Brock."

Brock didn't say anything for a moment. "I'm nothing special, Ryne. I'm just *normal*."

"Did you ever think maybe after all she's gone through within the phoenix clan, a more normal life might be what she needs?" With that, Ryne moved back to the door. "I gotta get back. The people need their wine. I know you'll remember who you are when the time is right."

"Like you said, the people need their wine." Brock shooed him out and shook his head with a small smile, but under his breath he said, "He's good people, but I think he might be wrong about me."

Brock arrived back at town square just as the peace ceremony was about to begin. He stood at the back edge of the group, observing the people who had arrived with their slips of paper filled with their anxieties, pains, and worries. He had taken a moment to fill out one himself, his anxiety now gripped tight within his fist. Most of the ceremony was unfortunately a blur for Brock as his mind was cluttered and his gaze kept involuntarily seeking out a certain redhead whom he didn't find. Even though he had promised himself he would stay away from her, he couldn't help but be disappointed that he didn't get to see her once more. Near the end of the ceremony, he said the prayer along with everyone else and lit his paper on fire, giving his anxiety to someone who hopefully had more power than he did to rid himself of his demons. On his paper he had written *insufficient*, and to his surprise, he felt a bit lighter watching it burn, the ashes dusting the thin layer of snow on the ground.

He headed back toward Soothing Sips to make sure all the cookies and hot cocoa along with their signature drinks were set up, and Macy, Gallad, and their dad, Reggie, had a good handle on things before he headed back to the winery. His mom, Lilith, and his grandma Eva, and Aunt Letti were serving cookies and cocoa at NamaStays Inn as one of the stops while he, Ryne, Hollis, Ruby Jean, and Brice (unofficially) manned the winery. However, before he got too far, Sunny found him and wrapped her arms around him from behind.

"Hey, Brock!" She giggled.

"Hello, Sunny. Are you working tonight's shift at Broastful Brew or do you get to enjoy the Cookie Crawl?" he asked.

She smiled up at him with her innocent blue eyes and big smile. "I have the night off. I'm going to taste the cookie competition and then end up back at the inn to help your mom and Aunt Letti. But before I go, a nice girl asked me to give you this box. It's so fun to get a surprise gift even before Christmas! It's something that will make your heart sing," she said with a suspiciously knowing smile.

"Did you open it, Sunny?" Brock playfully prodded.

Her mouth dropped in shock. "Of course not! I would never pry into someone's something special." She crossed her arms, offended at his suggestion then secretly smiled. "But I might have *seen* something in my special way, if you know what I mean." She made sure no one was near them then tapped her head.

Sunny had a gift similar to a seer's and could often see things in her mind's eye that related to the future. She had helped the Blackstones and others in the community on multiple occasions when she had first come to town. Her past was mostly still a mystery to everyone but Brice and those who needed to know, but Brock was not necessarily one of those. He, however, had found a special place in his heart to love Sunny and embrace her into their family as one of their own.

"Ah, I understand. Well, I should open it then," Brock said.

Sunny nodded and reached up and kissed his cheek. "I need to go. Embrace yourself. You already are you."

With that, she skipped off, careful to avoid a patch of ice, then went on her merry way.

Brock shook his head and smiled, "She's mysterious enough without the riddles. Am I supposed to hug myself?"

Instead he opened the small blue gift box, a blue that reminded him of certain phoenix eyes he was attempting to put out of his mind. No such luck. He pulled out one of the green and blue beaded mala bracelets the town had handed out for the peace ceremony. He had forgotten to grab one for himself and decided maybe it was unnecessary to have one. This one, however, was slightly different in the way it had a few extra charms attached. Spaced throughout the bead gems was a small charm of a silver bird with a long tail—a phoenix. Another charm: a reddish flame with streaks of gold, and the third a small blue sapphire. When the light hit it just so, it seemed to burn into a purplish color—the color of Chalise's eyes when they met his. This was from her. How could he put her out of his mind now? Or maybe that was the point. He couldn't help but place it on his wrist.

After visiting with several of the cookie crawlers, hearing various praise and comments on his and Brice's new holiday microbrew, and making sure his dad had everything under control at Sips, he headed back to the winery. He loved driving up to the winery at night any time of the year, but when a layer of snow blanketed the ground and gave an extra warm glow from the patio lights strung all about, it was simply magical. People still dashed around the town to all the designated locations to try all the cookies and consume all the cocoa they could before falling into a sugar coma, but quite a few already milled about the winery property since NamaStays Inn was also one of the stops.

Tonight was a huge boost for business and for the Blackstone Brothers Brews as well. He was so proud of all Brice had contributed to their growing business before he was of age and in the face of what Brice still had to learn about blending his hunter side with his witch side. Soon all that would change, and they could go full steam ahead.

Brock casually crossed the patio, stoking the fire pits and making sure the heat lamps were on, providing a warm area for extra seating. Already he saw familiar faces from town. A small group huddled around a fire at the far end looked up when he was close. He spotted Fin and Joe with Taylor and

Clay and waved. Near another fire were Rusty and Sherry. They raised their glasses to him.

Inside, a crowd was beginning to form, but it was still early. Jetta and Conrad sat in a corner near a window. Across from them were Karson and Scottlin; they gave him a salute with their glasses as he neared. Near the interior fireplace, Curtis Parker and Seamus Day shared a moment. Brock gave a wave to Ryker and Harlow who sat at the bar top, chatting with Hollis. Down a few seats from them sat Monte Tayute. He expected quite a few more to trickle in after the Cookie Crawl festivities came to a close. He waved to Ruby Jean, Ryne, and Hollis already manning the bar and serving the tables. He went straight to the back to have a quick meeting with Brice before it got too crazy.

"Hey, Brock, everything good at Sips?" Brice asked, looking up from the computer.

"Already bustling down there with the release from the ceremony. I think those not cookie hunting were so peaceful they wanted to keep the feeling going," Brock said with a chuckle. "Everybody is loving the new brew!"

"It's such a huge relief to have it out in the open. But I knew it would be a success!" Brice threw his fist in the air.

"I need to go check on Mom and the gals over at the inn before things get too busy and I forget."

"They've already called in their drink orders," Brice said with a laugh.

A knock at the door sounded before Hollis stuck her head through the opening. "Sorry to interrupt guys but, Brock, I have a delivery for you."

She handed him a blue sparkling envelope that instantly brought those same blue orbs that had been plaguing him for months to mind.

"Oooh, what is that?" Brice hopped up to lean on the desk corner to better see.

"None of your business," Brock countered.

"From a girl then?" Brice slapped his knee.

Brock looked up at Hollis. "She here?"

"Was, but then she left." Hollis gave him a knowing smile then left.

Brock stared at the envelope.

"Are you going to open it? Or just stare it?" Brice pushed.

Brock let the breath he'd been holding out of his lungs then opened it. Inside was a lighter blue paper with beautiful handwriting on it. It read:

Brock,

Before you walk away (which you have the option to do), I want you to know I see you. I see how much you love your town and your family. I see how easily you embrace those around you: Gallad the witch, Hollis a rogue hunter, Sunny the hunter/seer, Brice and his hunter/witch status and so many others. You see them for who they are and not just "what" they are. I'm asking for the same chance. You were one of the first I met and I knew then. I knew that you were someone I could trust and who would allow me to be who I needed to be. You are someone I feel safe with even with our limited contact. I'm asking for the chance for us to get to know each other with the potential for more. No pressure, just possibility. I found a place I think might be helpful. I know tonight is a big one for you and I think it could be even more. If you're willing, meet me at the old mine between Mt. Alexa and Mt. Sousa at seven o'clock.

Hopefully yours,
Chalise

"What's it say?" Brice asked, leaning forward, unapologetically butting into his brother's business.

"She wants to meet me…tonight. I can't go tonight. We have the launch…"

"Which I and the others are here for. Go meet her, bro."

"You don't understand... I'm not who she needs, I'm not..."

"Not what? Not good enough? Not sufficient enough? Not *man* enough?" Brice's voice rose with each question.

Brock stopped and truly looked at his little brother who was not so little anymore.

"Yeah, that's right. Every man about to enter into a relationship with the one of his dreams has those thoughts, those feelings. All it comes down to is: do you want her?"

"You had those feelings with Sunny? Even though you both are more than human?"

"Of course, bro. I mean, I don't go around advertising it, but yeah, I still do. But I'm not letting them stop me, because the end result is what I want, and I'm willing to work through my crap to get there. Are you?" Brice didn't back down.

"She could do better—"

"DO YOU WANT HER?" Brice cut in, yelling in Brock's face as only a brother could.

"Yes!" Brock shouted back before his brain could catch up with his words. He felt his body go into shock. "Oh my god, yes, I want her, and I think she wants me too. What is wrong with me?" Brock shook his head then looked around like he wasn't sure what to do.

"What the hell are you waiting for? Go get her and bring her back here in time for our launch!" Brice shouted with a big smile. And Brock rushed out the door.

Standing in front of a semi-boarded up old mine shaft, Brock's nerves faltered when he didn't see Chalise waiting outside. He stood there for several minutes talking himself out of continuing to wait for her. Five minutes past seven o'clock. She was late. But then his eye caught the glimmer off another sparkling envelope, this one white and easier to see in the dark. There was not much for light up this close to the mountain, but the glow of all the extra holiday lights from the town reflected on the snow. It wasn't enough to read the note, so he got out his cell phone and hit the flashlight button. He read the note.

"Follow my heart? What does that mean? Couldn't she say *Inside the mine. Careful it's dangerous.* Instead all I got was *Follow your heart and find your peace. I'm in the mine.*" Brock sighed with frustration and pointed his flashlight into the mouth of the dark mine. He held his breath and took the step inside, hoping he didn't fall to his death. The sounds of the town and all else instantly faded away. The air movement slowed, and he closed his eyes to try to orient himself.

A strange thing happened when Brock closed his eyes. He felt a tug on his heart and saw a vision of Chalise in his mind as if she was in front of him. Peace surrounded him like a warm blanket, and he wanted to follow where the pull originated. But that was crazy, right? He opened his eyes and breathed heavily in the dark entrance of the mountain. He felt bereft of her presence and longed to feel her once more. Mind made up, Brock closed his eyes and centered himself on the pull of his heart. He focused on it until he could still open his eyes and literally follow his heart. Holding out his flashlight so he didn't fall into a mine shaft, which thankfully were railed off, he slowly walked deeper into the mountain. When the feeling he followed grew so strong he almost couldn't breathe, he stopped and whispered her name.

"Chalise? Are you here?"

"You came," she said with the sound of relief. "I have to admit, it's a little creepy waiting in the dark inside a freaking mountain," she said nervously.

"Why did you pick this place? It's dangerous."

"If you'll turn off your flashlight for a minute, I'll show you. Just for a minute, because I want your eyes to adjust for the full effect." The excitement he could hear in her tone was contagious, so he clicked off his light to see what would happen.

"Before I turn the light on, I want you to just feel. Absorb the energy of the space around you. And tell me what you feel," Chalise requested as she pulled him a few more steps forward.

"All right." Brock closed his eyes once more and attempted to tune into his feelings. He felt Chalise's energy as she was next to him, so he reached for what else he might feel in the room. This wasn't something he would normally do, but for her, he tried. Brock inhaled then said, "Wow. I feel...I feel an overwhelming sense of peace. I feel positivity and clarity stronger than I ever have...and balance. Why do I feel all of this so strongly here?"

"When I say open, look down so the light is not too much at first." Chalise paused, then said, "Okay, go ahead and open your eyes toward the ground."

Brock did so and saw the light shining on the dirt, but then something else caught his eye as he followed the light as she moved it. Brock sharply inhaled at the magnitude of green and blue stones he saw roughly protruding from the cavern wall. The sight was something he would never forget. How did he—or everyone for that matter—not know this was here right next to where they lived and worked every day?

"Unbelievable. Is this amazonite?" Brock asked, lighting his flashlight in addition to hers to create an even bigger picture of the space they were in.

"Most of it; smoky quartz is mixed in. The amazonite for the bracelets—or the malas—for the ceremony today ultimately came from here. I had asked Hunter where he and Baba got the bracelets. He directed me to Madame Tahini; this is her secret. And as it's dangerous in a mine, she and Saundra Beaumont agreed we could come for a short time, but then asked us not to share this location with anyone."

Brock turned in a circle. "Thank you for bringing me

here." He purposely turned right into Chalise and gathered her in his arms before he lost his nerve. "Truly, you lured me here. I am grateful it was not to my death, unless that part's still coming." She laughed. Brock looked deep into her eyes, letting their depths consume him. "What you wrote in the letter… the part about choosing me, I need to know if that's true. I need to know you are not under any obligation to be with me."

Her response was decisive and right to the point. She leaned in and kissed him, full of desire and passion. He could feel the warmth of her phoenix rise to the surface, but instead of intimidating him or making him feel inferior, he wanted her to wrap him up in it. She broke the kiss all too soon.

"I have wanted you since the first day I met you, Brock Blackstone, mating bond or not. But I leave the choice in your hands," she solemnly said. Even in the dimmed light, he could see the red rimming her eyes begin to fade.

"I don't want to go another day without knowing you'll be in my life, Chalise. We have a long way to go and a lot to learn about each other, but I know without doubt I want to. I want to know you every day from this day forward. I may not have any supernatural powers, but I want to spend the rest of my life loving you, if you'll keep this foolish stubborn man around?"

"Then I think you have a date to your launch party tonight," she said with a smile.

"Then tonight is the first of many best nights!" he shouted as he picked her up and turned in a dizzying circle. Chalise laughed. Brock slowed them to a halt and nuzzled her neck, causing Chalise to swoon. "You may be a phoenix, but I am the one who has, out of the ashes of my insecurities, been reborn."

Merry Christmas from the Blackstone Family

Have you read all of the Blackstone Witch Hunters stories by Morgan Wylie?
Reawakened
Dawn of the Witch Hunters
Redefined
Rise of the Witch Hunters
Rediscovered

FINDING PEACE

BY SUSAN BURDORF

An Angelic Christmas Story

Cece opened the door to the Havenwood Falls Music and More store and flipped the sign hanging on the window of the entrance door to OPEN. The winter air was chilly, but not uncomfortably so, and she took a deep breath of the crisp, pine-scented air.

Havenwood Falls in winter was an amazing place, and the tourists who visited the area for its ski resorts and unique shops were plentiful as usual. Before stepping back inside the store, she waved to a few of the people passing by holding cups of coffee and some of the delicious blueberry scones from Coffee Haven, one of the most popular places in town to grab a cup to go.

She imagined Sherry would be stopping by in about 3... 2...1... The bell over the door chimed as it opened, and Cece turned, expecting to see Sherry with their morning coffee and scones, but instead a very well dressed, silver-haired man walked in then stopped, glancing around the store and looking a little lost.

"Hello," said Cece with a big smile. For the first hour of the store's opening, she was usually the only person in the shop until Glen or Mary came and she left for the Academy where she taught classes. But with finals approaching next week, there were no classes today, so she was here for a bit longer by herself. "May I help you?"

Cece gasped when he turned his face to hers. His eyes were dead inside. She was gripped and drawn into the intense darkness emanating from him. She didn't get the impression that he was dangerous, just that he was empty. His mind was closed to hers, but she probed gently and caught the flash of something—a face, a laugh—and then everything went shadowy and dark again, shuttered as firmly as if a door had closed and a lock engaged.

A woman. She'd caught the edge of an image of a woman, approximately his age, with silver hair and sunshine around her. Someone who'd mattered.

Before Cece could say anything, the man nodded, making the effort to give her a half-smile before he turned and stepped outside, striding away so quickly she almost let him go, but something told her to keep an eye on him.

Cece followed him out the door. Standing in front of the store, she frowned. Her eyes followed his progress until he disappeared into the crowd of tourists wandering around downtown Havenwood Falls. Every person he passed turned to look at him with a frown and a scolding comment about watching where he was going, and heads shook as they commented on his rudeness. It was as if his dark mood was affecting those around him.

"Why did he come into the shop and leave so abruptly?" she wondered aloud. He'd wanted something, had been drawn to her shop for a reason, and then was gone before she could reach out to him.

"Cece? You okay?"

Cece turned, a smile on her lips. She nodded to Sherry, who stood there holding two steaming cups of coffee and two paper bags with the Coffee Haven logo on them.

"I really need this today," Cece said. She wasn't sure if she meant the Coffee Haven treats or a visit from her friend. The two stood watching down the street after that man.

Sherry raised an eyebrow over the rim of her steaming cup of coffee. "Who was he?"

She nodded in the direction the visitor had taken when leaving her store. The tourists passing by were back to smiles and laughter, and Cece smiled in return.

Cece shrugged. Taking the top off the cup, she breathed in the welcome scent of peppermint-laced mocha, her favorite beverage at this time of the year. As an angel, she didn't really need to drink or eat, but when around human friends like Sherry, she would indulge in more human experiences.

"Come on back into the shop. I'm alone for the next little bit."

The two walked inside, and Cece took her place behind the counter while Sherry looked around the store. The two had known each other for several years now, and Cece marveled at how Sherry always seemed to know just what to do to soothe jangled nerves. Even an empath angel needed a muse once in a while, and Sherry was her wall of serenity.

Sherry knew what Cece was, and as the wife of Rusty Higgins, a local forest ranger and wolf shifter, she was also well aware that the town was inhabited by both humans and supernaturals. She and Cece had become fast friends, and Cece valued both Sherry's wit and her openness. Cece had a talent for spotting people who needed extra guidance and help when they were troubled by sadness or grief or other mental illnesses. Her talents were usually very subtly exerted to help maintain a person's equilibrium, but with Sherry, she didn't have to pretend to be anyone but who she was, and that was what made their friendship everlasting.

"He seemed to be in a hurry," Sherry said. Unwrapping the pastry, Sherry took a bite of the scone's gooey goodness and moaned. "These are the second-best part of Havenwood Falls," she said through a mouthful of scone.

"And Rusty is the first?" Cece chuckled.

"Well, sometimes…" Sherry winked.

Cece raised an eyebrow. "Everything okay?"

"Of course. We're doing fine. I just have a writing deadline, and he keeps distracting me."

"Ah, I see." Both women laughed. Rusty's distractions usually involved the bedroom, and Cece was happy her friend had someone to share her life with who fulfilled all her desires. Some were not so lucky.

"What about that guy? The one who ran out of here earlier. What's his story?"

Cece frowned as she opened the wrappings around her own scone a little more slowly. "I'm not sure about him yet. I didn't have enough time to really get a read on him. I could tell he's …" Cece shivered at the memory of the emptiness in his eyes and his mind. His heart had been broken, that was obvious to her, but by what? And what about that strange reaction from the people who'd passed him, almost as if his agony was transferring on to them, but how was that possible?

The woman she'd caught a glimpse of had been happy and full of sunshine. Could she be part of the darkness she saw in that man?

"Why did he come in here?" asked Sherry as she popped the last bit of the scone into her mouth.

"I'm not sure… yet." Cece handed her scone to Sherry, who was giving it a look of longing that brought a grin to Cece's face. "I have a feeling I haven't seen the last of him."

Just then the bell over the door jingled, announcing the arrival of a customer as an older woman and her granddaughter came into the shop. The granddaughter made a beeline for the row of popular music while the grandmother went to the retro section.

A few more customers entered, and Sherry gathered her things together. "Oh, I hear the Magic of Peace Ceremony will be amazing. Are you going?"

"Yes, I think so. I have one of the amazonite bracelets they are handing out." Cece held up her arm to reveal the pretty bracelet with its green stones. "And they left me some extra, which I put on the counter for the customers to take."

Sherry held up her wrist and laughed. "I have one too. I think they made enough for everyone in town to have one if they want it. I think it will be a great ceremony. We all need some peace right about now."

Cece nodded in agreement.

"Will that be all?" she asked as the grandmother and her granddaughter came up to the counter with their items.

"I'll catch you later," Sherry said as she picked up her coffee cup and headed toward the door. With a wave, she was out the door.

Cece was busy with a steady group of customers until her staff arrived and she could slip into the back office for some quiet time alone. She sat in the chair, contemplating the man who'd come into the store earlier.

Something about him was worrying her, and she couldn't quite put her finger on it.

Finally, in frustration she grabbed her jacket and headed toward the front of the store. "I'll be back in a minute," she told the young man at the cash register. "I just need some fresh air. You good here?"

"Yes, ma'am." Glen nodded as he smiled at the customer in front of him. He handed the woman her package, and she took her bag of goodies. Cece held the door open for her and was about to follow the customer out when she was struck by a deep cry for help that nearly took her breath away.

Cece leaned against the door, the cool glass soothing her brow as she considered where the cry had come from. Someone was in intense pain, so intense her hands were shaking in reaction to the connection.

What was that? she thought. *Who was that?*

Stepping outside, she held her breath for a count of three then blew out slowly. After a few seconds, the cries receded to the point where she could think clearly again. That was primal, and deep, and agonizing. Whoever was in pain, she needed to find them as soon as possible. That kind of pain led to only one thing, and she wasn't about to let that happen.

Glancing around her as she walked, Cece looked for anyone who appeared to be in distress, but couldn't find anything amiss. Everyone was smiling and happy. Chatter around her was full of the great skiing everyone was experiencing this December and how much they were looking forward to roasting marshmallows or lounging by the grand fireplace at the inn. Food was a topic on everyone's mind, and the children she passed were only thinking about Santa and what he might bring them.

A typical Christmas-season day in Havenwood Falls. Snow in the air, happy smiling faces, all the signs of a successful season for the town, and yet Cece could almost taste the urgent dread of that soul in distress. She knew she needed to find that person sooner rather than later.

Nodding to people she passed, she made her way around the square with little success. She couldn't find that person whose cry had driven her from the store no matter how gently she probed around the town.

Either that person is very good at hiding their emotions, or I am getting too old for this, Cece thought. Shaking her head, she was surprised to find herself in front of Coffee Haven and slipped inside. While not able to feel the temperature like humans did, she still enjoyed the warmth she imagined inside the coffee shop.

"Surprised to see you in here, Cece," a deep voice said behind her.

Cece smiled at Rusty, Sherry's husband, and said, "Oh, you know how it is. Even angels like coffee once in a while. It's a heavenly bean," she said with a chuckle, which Rusty echoed.

"Sherry would agree with you there. Matter of fact, that's why I'm here. I'm headed home for lunch, and Sherry asked me to pick her up a cup. She's deep into that book she's writing."

Cece rolled her eyes and smiled. Sherry's coffee addiction was a well-known fact around town.

"Rusty." Cece touched his arm to get his attention.

He looked back at her with a raised eyebrow. Brown eyes looked at her in concern.

"Everything, okay? You look a little worried." Rusty stepped out of line and pulled Cece to the side.

Cece frowned. Teeth nibbling her lip for a minute, she said, "I had a feeling earlier about someone in a… I'm not sure exactly how to explain it."

Rusty waited patiently.

"I…" she started and then the pain screamed out at her once more, only this time with such deep agony that she gasped and gripped Rusty's arm tightly.

"What is it, Cece?"

"We have to find him. He might do harm to himself or someone else, I'm not sure."

"Who?" Rusty glanced around the shop.

Cece couldn't see anything wrong as she followed Rusty's lead. No one looked like they were upset, but the screaming in her head didn't stop.

"I don't know where he is, but we have to find him. And soon," Cece repeated.

Rusty nodded. He knew of Cece's ability to distinguish those in pain. "My truck is parked right outside. Maybe we should drive around?"

"No time." Cece spun around and ran from the shop, bumping into people and apologizing as she made her way out the door.

When Rusty joined her, the big redheaded ranger gripped her shoulder. "You can't go running off not knowing what you are walking into. Let me come with you."

Cece shook her head then sighed. "It's gone. Whatever was drawing me has gone. But, Rusty, whoever that is, they are in deep pain, so deep I'm not sure I can help them come out again."

Cece glanced at Rusty, matching his worried expression with one of her own.

Dark eyes meeting hers, he said, "Do I need to be concerned about this? Should we let Sheriff Kasun know?"

"I don't think so. I think the danger is to the person themselves, and possibly to anyone around them when things go awry, but I get the impression that this person is suffering a personal pain, not one that is going to make them go ballistic or anything like that."

"Okay, I'm trusting you on this to let me know if I need to do anything."

Cece nodded. Heading back to the shop, she hated to admit defeat, but she couldn't find that person anywhere. Maybe they were better. Maybe the pain was fleeting, and everything was all right again. But she didn't think so.

The day flew by, and Cece was just getting ready to close up the shop when Sherry walked in. Her usual happy expression was a bit cloudy.

"Everything okay, Sherry?"

Sherry shook her head as if to clear her thoughts and gave Cece a weak smile. "Better now, but for a few minutes there, I was really upset. I have no idea why."

Cece set down the CDs she was returning to the shelves and pointed to one of the chairs she kept around the store for customers. "What's wrong?"

"I have no idea," Sherry said. She looked confused. "I was doing great, wanted to stop by and see if you would join me for a walk around the square to look at the lights after you closed the shop today when I started to feel tingly and then angry."

Now it was Cece's turn to look confused. "You didn't feel this way before coming here?"

"No, it happened before I got here. I was watching a crowd of kids tossing snowballs in the square and laughing and then I wasn't."

Sherry paused then continued with a confused expression, "There was an older man standing near me. He was staring at the kids with a very angry expression, and I thought he was going to say something mean to them, so I reached out and touched his arm. He turned to look at me, and that's when I got all weird inside."

Cece frowned. "Can you describe him?"

"He had white hair and wore a blue jacket, and he was... old. I couldn't really get a good look at him, but he kind of looked like the man who was in your shop today when I first got here."

Was that man the reason Sherry's mood changed so abruptly?

Cece looked at Sherry, and an idea popped in her head. "Can you take me to where you were? Before that, though, do you mind if I hold the hand that you touched him with?"

Sherry nodded. She seemed a little better. Cece held her friend's hand, but the impression of that man was faint. While a little of his essence lingered, it wasn't enough for her to get much of a read on.

"Let's go see if we can find him, okay?"

The two women walked toward the square where the

squeals of happy children echoed in the night air. Stars twinkled overhead like the Christmas lights dotting the trees and storefronts. Cece sent a small probe out to see if she could feel anything, and other than a few very vague impressions of darkness, she couldn't reach him.

She was certain now, more than ever, that this man who'd entered her shop that morning was the one calling out to her in his agony. Who else could it be? But why? Why had he sought her out this morning and then run from her?

"He's not here now," Sherry said, glancing around. She was right. Cece didn't see him, either.

The two friends decided to walk around anyway. Their conversations were filled with Sherry's gift ideas for Rusty and their plans for the holiday.

"I have one more gift to get him, but I just cannot decide what it should be," Sherry said.

Before Cece could answer with a few very adult suggestions, their conversation was interrupted by shouting. Glancing toward the other end of the square, the two noticed the man they were looking for arguing with another man.

Rusty stepped out of the shadows and moved between the two before whatever their argument was about erupted into violence. The white-haired man spun on his heel and hurried off in the opposite direction, disappearing before Rusty could grab a hold of him.

The other man shook his head and then responded to Rusty's questions with shrugs and hands in the air, gestures that implied he had no idea what had just happened. Rusty squeezed the man's shoulder once and then gestured for him to rejoin his family.

His eyes met Cece's and Sherry's, and he strode toward them with long, loping strides.

It was nearly time for him to go to the forest for his nightly rounds, but one last kiss with Sherry was in order, Cece noted with a shake of her head and a grin.

But while he did kiss Sherry on the cheek, he motioned for Cece to follow him apart from the crowds and Sherry.

"Cece, I think that was the man you're looking for. The gentleman he was arguing with says he has no idea what started it, and that he didn't even exchange words with the man, but once he was touched, he started to feel angry. He doesn't know why or what about."

Cece nodded. Looking in the direction the man had fled from Rusty, she couldn't see him. He was gone like a wraith. Reading him, she never had the impression he was dangerous, but if his anger was leaking out, that could be trouble. And Havenwood Falls didn't need trouble during one of its happiest seasons of the year.

"If you see him again, do you think you can hold him until I can talk to him?" Cece wasn't sure if Rusty would be allowed to do that. The man was human, and the rules were clear about interactions between humans and supernaturals.

Havenwood Falls protected the existence of its supes at all costs, but this man could not be allowed to ruin the season for others, and she was very concerned for his mental health and how it was taking over whenever he was around anyone else.

Rusty nodded. "I think in this case that is a good idea."

He waved to Sherry and Cece as he made his way across the square and into the nearby woods.

"That was him, wasn't it?" Sherry said.

Cece nodded. "I think so. He is in such deep distress, his mood is leaking out uncontrollably, and that could mean disaster for Havenwood Falls. I need to find him before he affects the mood of all our town's guests."

"You should bring him to the peace ceremony if you can," Sherry said. She tilted her head while thinking aloud. "I bet an amazonite bracelet will help heal him."

Cece looked at her bracelet and smiled. "That is a brilliant idea. I just need to find him now and convince him to join us there tomorrow."

❄

The morning of the peace ceremony was beautiful. Cece rearranged a few things in the store while she considered her next steps. There had been no more instances of unexplained angry outbursts, and Cece wondered where the man had stayed last night.

Welcoming customers, she barely had time to think about him. The shoppers were abuzz with talk about the Magic of Peace Ceremony and the Hot Cocoa and Cookie Crawl and several other events that would be happening in town over the next couple of weeks. Someone had stopped in at some point to refill the bowl with the bracelets for the ceremony, which had emptied again during the day. Cece slipped an extra one in her pocket, not sure why, but not questioning the impulse.

For a time, Cece forgot about the man.

But then, just after a customer left with their purchase, she felt the hard slap of his dark longing hit her. She gasped.

Leaning against the counter, she let the waves of his grief wash over her like a stormy ocean. The peaks and valleys of his pain became her pain, his darkness became her reality, and she couldn't think or move.

The image of a tree-lined path and a large rock assaulted her senses, and she knew where he was.

"I have to leave for a little bit. Can you cover?" Cece asked Gabriel Petran, Michaela's younger brother, who was restocking the albums.

He nodded, and she practically ran out the door, bumping into a few customers as she left and hurried toward Danzan Park. She hoped she wouldn't be too late. The throbbing in her head intensified the closer she got to where she knew she would find him.

Reaching the clearing, she saw a lone figure sitting on the top of the rock. He was huddled into a tight ball. He was sobbing, and the sound of his distress was gut-wrenching.

"Hello," Cece said softly as she approached him.

He didn't move or acknowledge her in any way. He continued to cry in that awful way that indicated hope was lost.

Cece moved closer until she could reach out and touch him, but she hesitated. He was in so deep, she wasn't sure her touch would rouse him from the place he'd gone in his mind.

She moved to stand in front of him.

"Hello, sir. Can I help you?"

He lifted his head. His face looked tortured by his grief. "Go away. Leave me alone. I need to be alone. I'll just make everything worse."

Cece moved closer. Touching his hands with hers, she said, "Let me help you."

He slapped her hands away and buried his head deeper into his knees. "I am no good to anyone anymore now that she's gone."

So I was right, Cece thought. *He is grieving someone.*

"Is this how she would want you to be?" Cece asked gently. She moved to sit by him on the rock.

He looked over at her. "Aren't you afraid my dark mood will make you angry too?"

She shook her head. "This is my favorite place to come and think. I sit on this rock and let the peace of the forest consume me. Don't you agree it's peaceful here?"

He glanced around. "I guess so."

"Was she your wife?" Cece asked after a few minutes of silence. Already she could feel the throbbing reduced to a dullness that bespoke her presence was calming him. But not enough, not nearly enough. He was holding onto that grief.

"Yes. Sixty years, until the cancer took her. We came here. To Havenwood Falls." He reached into a pocket and pulled out a small cat carved out of amazonite. "She'd wanted to come this year to get this blessed. I found a brochure for a town in Colorado, and then the name somehow changed to

Havenwood Falls. She'd marked it, and I felt drawn to come here."

"What did you do when you came?"

"We stayed in that cabin." He pointed into the trees. "This was our rock. We'd sit here for hours and talk. I didn't remember until I got back here."

"She's still here to you," Cece said. She looked at him, and he nodded.

"I miss her...so much," he whispered.

Cece patted his hand. The anger in him had definitely receded but was replaced by an emptiness that she wasn't sure how to refill.

"She loved you very much," Cece said. "Would she like to see you so angry?"

He shook his head. "Probably not. But that's all I have left. Anger. Sadness. More anger. It wasn't supposed to be her. It was supposed to be me first."

Cece nodded. She could understand his pain now. "My name is Cece. What's yours?"

"Randall. Randall Hancock."

"Nice to meet you, Randall Hancock. I am going to the peace ceremony. Why don't you come with me? You can get that statue blessed for her."

He followed her to the town square where the ceremony was being set up. Cece could see Baba and a few others decking the altar with the pine boughs and poinsettias. The bonfire was ready as well. She took a slip of paper from her pocket and handed it to Randall.

"Put on this anything you need to release to allow yourself to feel the peace of that memory," she told him as she handed him a pen.

"I don't want to forget her. I don't want to let her go," he said, hesitating to take the paper.

"You won't lose her memory," Cece said, touching his

heart. "She will always be there. You are just letting go of the pain."

Randall nodded. He wrote on the paper and held it tightly in his fist before handing Cece back her pen.

Cece noticed they had now placed the amazonite stone cat into the center of the arrangement. Candles were passed out for participants to hold, and bracelets given to those who needed them. Cece took the one out of her pocket and handed it to Randall. Mayor Barbie and Saundra Beaumont were in conversation with Baba then the mayor stepped forward to give a speech.

Arleta came around and lit everyone's candle from a larger one she held until all the candles around the square were lit. The lights brought a glow to the gathering that Cece found soothing and welcoming. She smiled at Randall, who smiled back. He held his candle in a trembling hand.

Cece squeezed his arm. The next part of the ceremony led to the sharing of wishes and hopes and dreams, and more prayers were said. Directions were given on what to do with the slips of paper, and people stepped forward to put them in the bonfire.

Randall hesitated. Glancing down at what he'd written, he cocked his head as if listening for guidance. A sense of true peace was already spreading over the square.

Cece watched Randall throw his paper into the bonfire before rejoining her.

He was smiling, and Cece found nothing in his mind that was disturbing other than a natural sense of grief and loss.

Sherry joined them a few minutes later and watched as Randall walked toward the man he'd earlier almost come to blows with. The two were soon laughing, and the man invited Randall to join him and his family for a meal and walk around town.

Randall looked over his shoulder toward Cece and nodded.

Thank you, he mouthed.

Then he was gone.

"He'll be okay?"

Cece nodded. "He'll be more than okay. Now, I think I hear a coffee calling our name, and the Hot Cocoa and Cookie Crawl is about to start. We better get a move on before all the good stuff is gone."

Sherry laughed. "You had me at coffee."

Merry Christmas from Cece, Sherry & Rusty

Read Cece's story in *Rock Me Gently* by Susan Burdorf

A REAPER'S CHRISTMAS VOW

BY JUSTINE WINTER

A Shade StormIron Christmas Story

"Happy Holidays!"

I nodded in response to the friendly woman as I walked through the town square, despite feeling more like Scrooge as the big day approached. I didn't know why, but this year I felt ready to reap all the souls who dared mention Christmas. Whether they were dying or not, they would be mine for the taking. Consequences be damned.

Like every year, Havenwood Falls sparkled and shined with twinkling lights and glittery decorations everywhere. It was like the man in the red suit woke up on December 1st and sneezed the season upon us. Ho-ho-ha-choo!

"Yo, Shade! Why didn't the reaper go to the Christmas ball?" a familiar voice called out to me. Her long, bright red hair flowed down her shoulders as she walked with a spry in her step.

"Christ, babycakes, where did you come from?" I shook my head at Nadine.

"Oh, you know, just around the corner, down the road, across the high street…"

"Yeah, I get it. Working on that stealth for college?" I raised a brow at the young Amazon. Getting Nadine into the Sun & Moon Academy College for Supernatural Guardians had been my most rewarding job yet. Whether she knew it or not, it was the best place for my misfit friend.

"Something like that." She winked. "So, you gonna answer my question?"

I stared at her blankly.

"Why didn't the reaper go to the Christmas ball?"

I sighed. "No idea."

"Because he had no body to go with!" She burst into a fit of laughter as though she'd been holding it in for some time. "Oh, come on. That's hilarious! You know, 'cause you're usually just a skeleton or black mist…"

I shook my head, letting a smile reach the corners of my mouth. She was just too infectious to ignore.

"How long have you been holding onto that lame joke?"

She crossed her arms over her chest, pouting. "A little while. You've not been around much at the college lately."

She gave me an accusatory glare.

"Been busy with work. I'm a highly important wanted man, you know."

"Yeah, yeah." She dismissed me with her hands. We continued to walk away from the town square, towards my place. At least, it was my place when I wasn't out collecting souls or helping at the academy.

"Everything all right with Thalia?" She raised a knowing brow at me.

"Perfect, never better. Except for all of…" I paused outside our house, which flashed brighter than New York City. "This!" I gestured to the herd of reindeer on the lawn, all moving to the same music popping out of Santa's ass like some hip hop video on Christmas crack.

"Wow..." Nadine exhaled. "Looks like she took it up a notch this year."

"Don't even get me started on indoors. It's..."

The door cracked open, and my beautiful forest nymph standing there took my breath away. How had I been so lucky?

"I thought I heard voices out here. Everything okay?" Thalia furrowed her brows and looked from Nadine to me and back again.

"It's all..." I paused, a familiar feeling vibrating on my wrist and working its way through my body. "Uh-oh. Sorry ladies..."

Nadine and Thalia looked at one another and said in unison, "He's gotta go."

I laughed loudly as I was pulled away, my body changing to mist as my form disappeared. It was the deal I'd made with the WitchHound Addie: her tattoo gave me a skinsuit but didn't stop me from reaping. When a soul called, I changed, and I followed the song wherever it took me.

I transported in darkness, nothing to see as my spirit instinctively knew where to take me. I bumped from side to side as turbulence took hold. The soul was near, its essence calling out to me. I readied my chains as I zapped through a portal into what looked like Cornwall, England. The sun had long set, and the coast was quiet in the distance; only the ebb and flow of the waves could be heard faintly.

After reaping for more than 200 years, there was little of the world I hadn't seen before—and some places more often than others.

I hovered in the sky, looking over the scene below. Blue lights flashed, voices yelled with commands, and above it all, screams and sobs came from a woman leaning over a body covered in a white sheet. It was something I'd seen too many times to count. A loved one gone too soon. An accident where only one survives of a family in a car crash. They didn't get easier either—human deaths were the worst. The souls always felt lost.

I swooped down, knowing I couldn't be seen by anyone but the soul hovering above the body in confusion. I cuffed it to me before it knew what was happening and opened another portal to the afterlife—a place where souls could rest in peace. It was the exact opposite of the Infernum. There were no screaming walls, raging fires, or the worst of the worst creatures imprisoned together. The afterlife was calm, serene, and tranquil. I unbound the soul once we made it through and left it to find its own path here. It was what I liked most about this place. The souls needed little attention and energy from me. I was just their glorified transportation.

I took off for home, knowing there was a certain sexy lady waiting for snuggles. I zapped through the portal and into another. A loud boom throbbed in my head, and I was falling, losing all momentum in my wings. I scraped against jagged walls, and brimstone filled the air like a fart bomb. I landed with a thud, and a cloud of dust enveloped me.

"Merry Christmas, Shade."

I groaned, trying to stand up.

"So nice of you to pop in and see me in this festive season."

I silently cursed to myself. I should've known what was happening the minute I lost control of my body—there was only one guy who had control over me.

Ahead, dressed in an all-green suit, sitting in his favorite throne surrounded by flames billowing from concrete stands, was Death. He'd never looked so merry and Christmassy before. Was he going through some kind of mid-life crisis? This was not normal, and completely unnerving.

I flexed out my bones, adjusting myself. "I thought I'd drop your Christmas gift off." I winked, pointing at my skeleton frame. "You're welcome."

"That's not much of a gift, considering I already own

you," he grumbled. If I didn't know better, I would've thought he was seriously disappointed. Luckily, I knew he didn't give a shit. "Perhaps you could give me something else instead?"

I leaned forward, sensing a trap. "What can I give you, other than souls?"

Death stretched out his large hands, placing them on his lap, a menacing grin covering his face. "Your loyalty."

I remained silent, waiting for the punch line. There was no way he was serious—I didn't have any choice but to give him my loyalty. He was the only one who could rid me of my existence. I lived to do his bidding, and I served him well. Didn't I?

"Cat got your tongue, Shade? You're usually so witty with retorts."

"I, um…" I paused. Was I really speechless? "I'm not sure what you mean…"

"Ha!" Death leaned forward, pounding his hand on the arm of the throne. Vibrations rattled around the room, the ground shuddering beneath my feet. "It's simple really," he urged.

"But you already have it."

Silence hung in the air like a dense fog, thick and suffocating.

"How can I be so sure when you're spending so much time in that supernatural town of yours?"

A lightbulb switched on in my mind, and I suddenly realized why I was struggling with the holiday season. It was like an epiphany, and I knew what I had to do.

"How can I prove my loyalty to you if the fact I'm still reaping souls for you isn't enough?"

Death leaned down toward me. His large head was bigger than my body and took up all of the space.

"There are trials you must pass. If you succeed, I will no longer question you."

"And if I don't?" I stared into his onyx eyes, losing myself in the dark abyss.

"Well, I'll have no need of you...." He let his sentence hang in the air, the unfinished words enough to understand.

"What are the trials?"

"That is for you to find out."

I inhaled, seeing my choices were limited. Death would put me through it whether I wanted to or not, but there was something I could get out of it...

"If I do this, and succeed, I want you to give me free reign to live within Havenwood Falls indefinitely. No ifs, ands, or buts. After this, you can't take it all away from me."

Death receded back to his throne, putting his hands to his lips in contemplation. I'd made myself completely vulnerable to him. I couldn't enjoy the festivities knowing he could take away my Havenwood Falls life with a flick of his fingers. I couldn't live in limbo like that anymore. Not when the longer I stayed, the deeper my roots settled with the people I'd grown to love.

"Fine," Death spoke, disrupting my thoughts. "Prove your loyalty once and for all, and you'll have your wish."

I waited, knowing it wasn't final yet. Not without a promise; I'd seen the big guy con a lot of fools in my lifetime.

"You have a deal," Death confirmed.

"What do you mean 404 page not found? You stupid piece of shit." I banged the keyboard.

Ding, ding, ding.

"Don't you sass me back!" I shouted at the computer as it continued to beep at me. "You know, you're only as smart as the humans who built you."

"Geez, are you trying to use it or kill it?" Thalia stood in the doorway, leaning against the frame.

"I thought this thing was supposed to know everything?" I sprang out of the chair, frustrated with the new-age machine. Compared to it, I was ancient.

"I haven't seen you this worked up in a long time." She wrapped her arms around my neck, pulling her body flush against mine. How was a man to concentrate with her so close?

I claimed her lips, letting her spicy vanilla scent surround me. She was warm and supple where I was cold and solid.

"What's going on, Shade?" She held me close so I couldn't escape her grasp—she knew me too well.

Did I tell her about my deal with Death knowing there was a chance I could fail? Though I believed I had full loyalty to Death, the trials wouldn't be fool-proof, whatever they were. What would Thalia think if she knew I'd basically put our life together on the line? How much did she care about me? About us? Was she as ready to commit as I was? Our relationship had gotten off to a rocky start, and she was fragile when it came to intimacy. But now, she was so much more confident.

"I was trying to do some research." I sighed, knowing I'd been quiet for too long.

"Something for the academy?" She piped up, releasing her hold and stepping around me. "Death trials?" she enquired as she read the web page URL I had tried to open. Confusion and concern marred her voice. "Something going on with your reaping?" She turned to look at me, brows furrowed.

"Not quite," I hedged.

"What aren't you telling me? And don't even think about placating me with your charming bullshit."

Shit, she was mad. When her hands landed on her hips and nostrils flared, I knew I was in trouble.

"Death is questioning my loyalty since I came here and built a life for myself. So I'm proving him wrong." I shrugged like it was no big deal. Truth was I'd never heard of any trials being done before. I was completely in the dark.

"And you think the answers are online?"

"Possibly," I mumbled, feeling like a scorned child. "No harm in looking." I skulked. What else could I do? Reapers didn't exactly have a social network to keep connected—Skullbook didn't exist yet.

"What now, Shade? I'm guessing this doesn't end in a happily ever after if you fail!" Thalia yelled, face reddening with anger.

"I don't know!" I stormed away, hitting the stupid Christmas decorations out of the way. The bloody place was like a Santa-approved assault course. I slammed the front door shut behind me, taking a deep breath of crisp, fresh air. It was cold, but pleasant. I made my way through town, walking aimlessly, ignoring everyone who dared come close enough.

An exhilarating chill shuddered along my spine. My bones cracked, and organs and skin melted away effortlessly as my wings released and the call of a soul overtook my senses. Time ceased to exist as I careened through darkness like I was being sucked into a vacuum. If I had my skin suit on, my organs would be like lumpy tomato soup oozing out of my belly button.

"Stop." The command blasted through me. A force of power kept me still. I tried flexing a bony digit, but I couldn't move. I was stuck.

What the hell was happening?

Darkness surrounded me. Wherever I looked, there was nothing to be seen. I was alone, yet I could feel an energy nearby, hovering in the distance.

"You know, if you wanted to ask me out on a date, you could've sent a message instead," I joked, trying to coax whatever was out there a little nearer so I could see what I was dealing with.

Silence.

I tried moving, but I was still trapped, like glue was holding me in place.

"Aw, come on. Don't be such a tease," I urged.

Gravity pulled me down, and wind whipped around me as I was freefalling. I tried engaging my wings, but it was like they were clipped; I couldn't sense them.

Was this Death's doing? A part of his trials? I hated not knowing what to expect. I didn't even know when they'd start or how many there were. I had zero clue. As much as I could tell from my lack of successful research, Death's loyalty trials were unheard of. What the hell was going on? I couldn't feel the soul calling me anymore either. In fact, I couldn't really feel anything.

I was numb.

Loud, thumping music rattled my bones. Every now and then soulful Christmas music blared out. It was Death's rendition of the human's seasonal classic Christmas song. Slowly, I stood, joints stiff from the cold air blasting above me. Where was I?

I stepped forward, hoping to get a better view. Metal bars stopped me in my tracks. I turned, seeing they surrounded me. I was in a cage. Sulphur cloaked the air like an evil perfume.

"Get out!" A roar rumbled through me, and I instinctively moved. I frantically searched the bars for a doorway but found none.

"Screw this," I mumbled to myself and grabbed two bars. I inhaled, readying myself, and using all my strength, pulled the bars apart. There was so little resistance I'd almost dislocated my elbows with the force.

"That was...unexpectedly easy," I said, wary as I stepped out of the cage. A bright green hue appeared, shining around me, like I was being lit up. I didn't like it. This spotlight put me at a huge disadvantage. I still didn't know who my enemy was here.

I kept my guard up as I walked toward the light, my wings still strangely absent.

I didn't like it; my senses were all messed up. I tried opening a portal to get back to Havenwood Falls, but it seemed like all my powers had gone.

A large wooden door appeared before me. It towered over me, and a large iron knocker stared back at me. Gingerly, I reached out, expecting something negative to happen the moment I touched the handle.

Nothing…

I turned the knob, and the door swung open with a loud creak. I waited, anticipating…something. Again, nothing happened. None of it made sense. The loud obnoxious Christmas song had gone, though not for long. Next up was another Death rendition of Silent Night called Soulless Night. It was like some cheesy Deathmas karaoke competition going on.

This was all completely bizarre.

I moved forward, looking for some kind of way out of this weird maze-like darkness. A large tombstone appeared before me, my name written over it in some fancy chicken scratch writing. The date was set to today, 18th December 2021. Was this it? Had Death finally had enough of me and this was his way of telling me? Was he not going to give me time to say goodbye to Thalia? To Nadine? Hell, not even a flick of a finger to WitchHound Addie as a parting gift goodbye?

How was I supposed to fight this when I had no control over what was happening?

A loud boom cracked through the air. Pieces of stone crumbled to the ground as I watched a gate appear in the center of my tombstone. I lifted the latch, took a deep breath, and stepped through. It was all eerily quiet. No more Christmas songs, but a light shone on a thin podium. It stuck out of the ground, and a green hue shone on top of it. Curious, I stepped closer and realized the hue of color was actually an object. It was small with jagged edges. Was it a gem? I picked it up, and the ground disappeared beneath my feet, and I was falling again.

"Shade!" Death's unmistakeable voice greeted me as I landed with a thud, the gem still clasped in my bony hand.

I hurried to my feet and gasped. "What the fuck happened here?"

I stood open-mouthed, flabbergasted to see the usual sparse, dark, flame-lit room was covered in red and green tinsel, lights, and even a twenty-foot Christmas tree decorated with baubles.

And, more disturbingly, Death sat in his throne wearing a red suit and Santa hat.

A bloody Santa hat!

Something was very wrong.

"Come now, Shade. Don't you feel like celebrating?" Death smirked.

"Since when do you celebrate Christmas? You're more of a Halloween man."

"That's true. I do revel in trickery." He chuckled, and the walls shook with his loud tone. "But I'm getting quite merry, 'cause you, my loyal Reaper, passed the trial."

I waited for the punchline. None came. "I did?" I frowned. "When?"

"Just this minute."

"But what did I do?" I was perplexed. I expected to be huffing, puffing, and close to death when I took the trials.

"You stepped over the threshold without resistance. Only someone who was truly loyal would be able to escape the cage like that."

"What do you mean? All I did was pull the bars apart?" It hadn't been rocket science, but Death seemed to be making out that it was still a big deal. Why?

"Shade, my mentally challenged fool. If you hadn't been completely loyal to me, the bars would not have opened so easily. Actually, they wouldn't have opened at all, and it would've been quite painful…" He paused. "Scratch that, not painful, but you would've died there and then."

"WHAT!" I yelled, astounded. I'd been completely oblivious. "You didn't think to mention that to me before?"

Death shrugged. "Why? So you could *pretend* to be loyal to me? What good does that do me? The spell doesn't work like that. It seeks out your true intention. Come now, Shade. What's there to worry about now? It's done. Quick, easy, and simple. You should be happy!"

Holy shit, if Thalia had known…

I wasn't so sure *happy* was the right adjective to use. Relieved, yes, but happy? I hadn't known what to expect, but I'd assumed something much more exhausting, challenging, and time-consuming was in the cards. I almost felt cheated, like I'd been psyching myself up for something that never happened.

But I'd known I was loyal. So why was I so surprised? Humans believed God worked in mysterious ways, but Death had him beat in that.

I thought back to the craziness I'd just endured. "If getting out of the cage proved my loyalty, what was with all that other crap afterwards? Why did I see my tombstone?"

"Oh, that was me just fucking with you and having fun." He laughed maniacally, clearly enjoying himself.

"So our deal is done?" I raised a non-existent brow.

He nodded. "I believe you are holding the amazonite crystal, are you not?"

I lifted my hand, revealing the green stone. "This means I'm free to stay wherever I please without you taking it all away from me?" I still didn't trust that I'd done it.

"It does." He nodded solemnly. "Though you will continue to reap."

I nodded. I wasn't sad about that. I quite liked my purpose and job.

"Oh, and Shade? Don't make me regret giving you this. You should know by now, I don't give free passes to just anyone."

"Are you sure I'm doing the right thing? We didn't exactly leave things on the best of terms before my trials," I asked Nadine as we stood outside Coffee Haven. The town was busy with last-minute holiday shoppers.

"You're joking, right? Thalia loves you, she has to, to put up with your random disappearances. She knows the score with your reaping, but what you're about to give her will more than make up for it."

"You sound pretty positive there, baby cakes. I'm almost convinced." I winked, staring inside the small jewelery box. "Did she say anything to you when I disappeared?" Christ, I was like a teenage girl fishing for answers. I hadn't ever been so nervous before.

"Enough for me to know you'd be stupid not to do this."

I nodded, filling myself up with courage. "Okay, wish me luck."

"You don't need it, not when you tell her where the stone for that ring came from. Laters, dude." She tapped my arm and walked away, leaving me to walk into Coffee Haven alone. I knew it wasn't romantic, but it was the scariest shit I'd ever done, and I wasn't about to back out now.

Sitting in the corner of the shop, sipping what I was sure would be a hot chocolate laced with fresh mint, was the most beautiful woman I'd ever met in my 200-plus years. She was everything to me, everything I hadn't known I wanted until I'd met her dancing on a stage in Silk.

"Thalia," I called, loving the way her name rolled over my tongue.

"You're back," she exhaled, surprised. "You were gone for days…"

"I know, and I promise I'll explain everything, but there's something I have to ask you first." I could sense she wanted to argue, but there must have been something in my face that held her back.

"Did you pass?" she whispered, clearly understanding why I'd been gone so long. Her trust in me overwhelmed me every time.

I nodded. "I did. Thalia…" I stepped down on one knee, forgetting everyone else inside the coffee shop. I couldn't wait any longer. I pulled the small box out of my pocket and opened the lid to reveal a ring with the green stone from Death—the one that signified my freedom, my peace—in the center. The jeweler had carved it into a tear drop and placed glistening diamonds all around and set it above a double band with the words *'you have my soul'* carved into it. I was willingly giving everything I was to Thalia.

She gasped, tears sparkling in her eyes.

"Thalia, will you marry me?"

Merry Christmas from Shade, Thalia & Nadine

Read Shade and Thalia's story in *Damned Allure* by Justine Winter.

ENDINGS & BEGINNINGS

BY KRISTIE COOK

An Addie Beaumont Yule Tale

"Adelaide," Saundra Beaumont greeted me as I entered the office she kept at Sun & Moon Academy College of Supernatural Guardians as one of the local Regents. She sat behind the bare desk, her arms folded on top of it, wearing her typical business suit with her silver hair in its normal twist. Goddess, I hoped I didn't become as boring as she was in my old age. "Any news?"

"Grandmother," I said as I strode up to the chair in front of her but didn't sit. Ignoring her question, I asked my own. "You wanted to see me?" I held the parchment in my hand with her elegant handwriting scrawled across it, requesting a meeting. It had appeared out of thin air and floated down to my own desk a few minutes ago.

She gave a short nod. "I do, but not now."

My brows furrowed. "Then why are you here? On campus, I mean."

She only taught a couple of classes, so she wasn't here

often, but now the semester had ended, and students were packing for the break as we spoke.

"Why are you?" she countered, but she didn't let me answer. "You've been spending an unusual amount of time here on campus. More than necessary for your teaching duties." I only responded with a shrug. "I understand why. The end of the second lunar cycle is next week."

My jaw clenched. As if I needed the reminder. "I'm fully aware."

Her dark gaze traveled over my face, snagging on my tightly pressed lips. "No news is good news, Adelaide."

I gave the slightest of nods, inhaling a breath before responding any further. "Is this what you wanted to talk to me about? To remind me of a deadline I can't escape even if I tried?"

"We do need to discuss it, among other things. But not now. I'm only here to ensure campus closes for the winter break without any…issues like we've experienced in the past."

I suppressed a snort. "Issues" was an understatement. Although last year and this past semester hadn't been quite as eventful as the opening year of the college, the campus continued testing its students in the most dangerous of ways. Fortunately, nobody had died since that first year.

"You'll be coming to the coven's Yule Ceremony?" Her voice lilted at the end, as though making it a question, but her expression said it was not.

"You know I prefer honoring the day and celebrating solo," I said. When it came to fighting dangerous threats to our town and my people, I was more than happy to join my powers with other witches and usually led the charge. But for rituals and ceremonies, I preferred my solitary practice rather than mingling with the Luna Coven. Especially these days.

Saundra pursed her lips. "Come to my home on Sunday, four o'clock sharp. We have much to talk about."

"Including why you've reduced how many classes I teach

by half?" I challenged. Anger still churned in my chest about that, which was one reason I felt so defensive today. The teaching schedule I'd been given for next semester only had me on campus for two days a week.

"You have other responsibilities," she said, not needing to remind me of my obligations to the Court of the Sun and the Moon as their business manager. "That was not entirely my say, though, and you know that. You're a member of the Board of Regents yourself."

True. But they'd outnumbered me when I asked for more classes. If I had my way, I'd be on campus full time. It was better than the alternative future I faced. I didn't get my way, though. The members of the Court who were also Regents made sure of that. Of course, they'd also appointed me as Provost, leader over all of the deans, a so-called promotion, but one that had me less engaged with students and more involved with the other Regents and the Court. More involved in the politics, in other words. Yuck. No matter how hard I tried to pursue a different path, they seemed hell-bent on putting me in leadership.

"For now, see to it that the students who are remaining behind for the holidays are taken care of and the rest leave campus and town safely," she said, her tone dismissing me.

Already planning to do just that, I returned to my office to gather my belongings. Before leaving, I flicked my hand to straighten anything out of place and turn off the lights, but as expected, only a wadded-up piece of tissue moved—and barely a flutter at that. Blowing out a frustrated breath, I tossed it in the can like a Muggle. I didn't know what was wrong with me and was just thankful that Saundra hadn't needed me to use my magic for anything. Because lately, it seemed non-existent. On the other hand, if she knew my issues, she surely wouldn't care so much that I attended the Yule Ceremony. Maybe I should tell her after all.

Switching on my professor face and demeanor, I jogged

down the stairs to the main floor of Halstein Hall, where the student union was located. A few stragglers remained, but it appeared that most of the students had already cleared out for the break. After speaking with the skeleton crew that would stay behind for those students who didn't have a home to go to for the holidays—or just didn't want to leave—I crossed the stone courtyard of the underground campus and looked back one more time before passing through the archways that led to the bridge.

I loved this campus with its enormous stalagmites and columns that housed the dorms and classrooms, lights still glowing in some of the windows and doors carved into the stone. The fact that it existed at all was proof enough that magic was real. If the human world knew about this place under the mountain, it would certainly be in the running for one of the main wonders of the world.

Crossing the bridge over the underground river, I passed the Valkyries that stood guard and headed toward the vestibule that housed the portals. The bottleneck from earlier, when the last of final exams let out, had dissipated, now only short lines at each portal.

"See you next year, Professor Beaumont," one of the freshman witches said, waving at me.

"Enjoy your holidays," I replied before she stepped into the portal that would take her to the campus of the SMA high school on the edge of town. From there, her family would meet her, and she'd be headed to her home in Florida for a few weeks. I was surprised to realize that I envied her. I was not surprised, however, as the last of the students disappeared into the portal, with just how much dread filled me as I neared the magical gateway myself.

I loved my town as much—no, more than—I loved the campus. I was born and raised here, and this would always be my home. My grandmother had sent me around the world while I was growing up to learn various magic and develop and hone my powers, and I appreciated the opportunities and experiences. But there was no place like Havenwood Falls.

Lately, though, it hadn't felt quite…right. Like something was wrong. Or missing. Or, truthfully, *someone* was missing. I'd hoped the Magic of Peace Ceremony last weekend would have relieved the feeling, but it hadn't. Not for me.

My chest tightened as I approached my home on the north end of town, a couple of blocks from town square. It just hadn't felt the same since…since the day after Samhain. So much emptier now. The very reason I'd been spending so much time on campus.

The sadness eased, though, when a large wolf came from around the side of the house and trotted up to me, tail wagging as his tongue lolled out the side of his mouth in a wolfy grin.

"Chewie!" I greeted, wrapping my arms around my familiar's neck and sinking my fingers into his silver fur. "I missed you, too."

A raven cawed from a branch just overhead.

"Yes, I missed you, as well, Skywalker," I said as he landed on my shoulder. "I'm sure Kylo and Princess Leia missed us all."

The tuxedo cat eyed us from his favorite windowsill, pushing himself to all fours and arching his back in a stretch before he disappeared, presumably to greet us at the door. When I opened it, Princess Leia, the miniature dragon who wasn't much bigger than Kylo Ren flew into the entry and circled overhead.

"I know, I know," I said, dropping my things in the living room. "I've been gone a lot, but I'm home for a few weeks now. Well, the Court has things for me to do, and I'm guessing by Grandmother's demeanor today that she has demands as well, but I'll be here to sleep at least."

I chatted with them the rest of the afternoon while I watered my plants, cleared the stale energy in my home with some sage smoke followed by copal, and then did a little decorating for the holidays. My home would no longer be the only one in the whole damn town that wasn't lit up. One of the best things about my familiars, besides the fact that they could share their magic with me, was that they were good listeners. And not once did they ask, like everyone else in this busybody town always had for the last seven-plus weeks, where Tase was or if I'd heard from him.

Well, I was wrong. Princess Leia wanted to know. She didn't ask, of course, being a dragon, but she incessantly flew from room to room, searching for him and Carter, Tase's son. Probably more for Carter, since they often played together. My heart squeezed at the thought of the boy. I'd struggled at the whole stepmother role, but I kicked ass at being an auntie. As I reluctantly slid out of the driver's seat of my jeep and trudged up the walk to Saundra's mansion in Havenwood Heights Sunday afternoon, I could only hope it was all worth it for Carter.

"You're early," Saundra said as a greeting before leading me from the foyer and down the hall.

I sighed as I followed her. Sometimes I felt like I could never please the woman. As we took our seats in her home office, I knew I wasn't here as her granddaughter. Although it was Sunday, this was obviously about Court or coven business.

"You just turned twenty-nine. It's your Saturn return," she said from behind her desk, folding her hands in her lap. "It's expected that you would sabotage your relationship and your life."

I blinked, my mind going blank for a moment before trying to process what she meant. Shit. I hadn't even thought about it being my Saturn return, but she was right.

"Hold on," I said. "You think I *sabotaged* my relationship

and my life?" My grandmother was not a typical grandma type with freshly baked cookies, a warm shoulder to cry on, and reassuring words to provide comfort and love. Obviously. But this was just...cold.

One of her thin shoulders lifted. "The Saturn return comes every twenty-nine years or so, and they're rough. Especially the first one."

No stranger to astrology, I knew what the Saturn return was—when Saturn revisited the sign it was in at the moment of one's birth, bringing intense energy with it. It happened once every twenty-nine years, give or take. I'd heard the cautionary tales about other people's returns, particularly their first ones. Decisions were often made that were literally life changing. New jobs or total career switches, moving across the country or around the world, buying a home, getting married...or ending long-term, committed relationships. The first time supposedly brought that change of energy necessary to transition from a young adult still trying to find their place in the world to settling into that place and taking on responsibilities of being a grown-up. It tended to be a difficult time for most, resulting in some kind of upheaval before the settling occurred.

Sabotage, though? My life had definitely taken a different direction than I'd expected a year ago, but had I really sabotaged it? Was that what other people thought?

"I've been through several returns myself," she said, "but thank Goddess, they do come easier each time."

I blinked again. I'd never really considered how many of these potentially life-changing celestial events my grandmother had been through. Most people experienced two, around twenty-nine years old and then fifty-eight, and those who lived long enough had a third, around the age of eighty-seven. But witches and other supernaturals, of course, lived through many.

"I'm not sure, however," Saundra continued, "that I'll see my next one. It's coming up in three years or so."

"Wait. *What?*" I temporarily forgot about the whole sabotage thing. I leaned forward as that sense of dread I'd been carrying for weeks deepened. "Grandmother, what are you saying? Is something wrong?"

She inhaled slowly while staring at the desk's surface before lifting her eyes to lock on mine. "I've been feeling a little…off, Adelaide. Different. Perhaps it's nothing. But if it is, that is fine. I've lived a long time already. I'm not really sure I want to go through another Saturn return…or any other returns, for that matter. It all becomes a bit tiring after a while. A little monotonous."

I stared at Saundra Beaumont, not knowing what to say. This woman—High Priestess of the Luna Coven, esteemed member of the Court of the Sun and the Moon, matriarch of the Beaumonts for nearly a century-and-a-half—this woman was a *rock*, not only of our family but for the whole damn town. She'd only been a toddler at the time, but she'd been part of the group who discovered the box canyon! Although I'd been groomed to eventually take those same leadership roles at some point in the future, I'd never actually considered her being…gone.

She cleared her throat and flipped a hand in the air dismissively, her tone returning to normal when she spoke. "Well, I didn't mean to bring that kind of energy into this meeting, but it is somewhat relevant to why I wanted to talk to you today."

"Because you're *dying*?" I nearly snapped.

"No need to be so dramatic, Adelaide," she replied drily as she leaned back in her chair. "I'm not dying. Not as far as I know, anyway. But I do believe that my time in this world is coming to an end, and it's time to start accepting that will happen at some point and to plan for it. I don't expect to be on the Court much longer or serve as High Priestess of the coven, either."

My breath caught. "Grandmother—"

She cut me off. "Whether I live for another two years or fifty-two, it doesn't matter. It's time for new blood. Michaela has shown that for the Court, and with everything that has happened with the Collector and Zandra and Kialah…" She paused, sharply exhaling. "We started the college and training of an army for a reason. And they need new leadership. Many of us are aware of that now. I don't believe I'm the only one considering stepping down."

I didn't know what to say. I honestly never thought I'd see this day. Hear what I was hearing.

"You've talked to Mom about this?" I asked.

She nodded. "Yes, which is why I'm talking to you now. About your Saturn return and you sabotaging your life."

I slumped back into the chair, suppressing a growl at the reminder. "I haven't sabotaged my life."

"Did you not just let Atanase walk out of your life when not so long ago you were *fighting* for his life and your love?"

"You know why he left. There was an entire Court meeting about it, and you were among the others who agreed it was best for everyone, including Carter."

Her brows pinched, and she glanced away. While I wasn't sure how secretly glad she was to have Tase out of the picture —particularly my picture—I knew she missed that little boy, her great-grandson, even if she only had a couple of years with him. She returned her dark gaze to me. "I'm just surprised you let Atanase leave so easily. Or do you not love him anymore?"

I sighed internally. There was more to the story than that, more to it than anyone could know. Well, besides Xandru and Michaela, and Rhian, of course. Letting Tase leave with Carter was probably the hardest thing I'd ever done—and the most necessary. The public story was that Havenwood Falls didn't provide a good environment that allowed Tase to be the best father he could be. Not when he was constantly roped in by the Bishops to do their dirty work or tempted by his younger siblings to protect the Roca (dis)reputation. He needed a fresh start away from this town, including me. That was the story fed to the gossip mill. But the truth involved Zandra, the Collector, and secret intelligence indicating Carter's life may have been at risk here.

The one place that should have been a safe haven for him, like all other supernaturals, was possibly the most dangerous.

We didn't tell the Court everything we'd learned from our source—we hoped none of it ever came to pass—but just enough for them to agree to a small loophole in the town's rules. That Tase was given two lunar cycles instead of one before he lost his memories plus a talisman, in case he ran into trouble that he couldn't handle on his own before he got to safety. I spelled the talisman myself to create an emergency portal for him to return with Carter.

I felt Saundra's expectant eyes on me, waiting for some kind of response.

"Love is not always enough, Grandmother." I paused, mentally debating whether to remind her of how she'd treated my parents when they found out Mom was pregnant. She'd told them something along the same lines. "And you know I couldn't exactly go with him."

"Couldn't you have?"

"My home is here. I can't *leave* Havenwood Falls. Not for good. You know that better than anyone." After all, she'd been the one to drive that point into my brain since I was four years old, and I had a gut feeling that was why I was here today— for her to swing the hammer once more, making sure that nail was not only embedded but buried.

"Speaking of...I want you at the Yule Ceremony. Since you've made this choice, it's time you start taking a more active role with the coven. I am asking if you will lead this year's ceremony."

I tried not to squirm in my seat, knowing she'd only reprimand me for it. I was twenty-nine years old and still got in trouble for not acting properly for someone of my "station." But if there was any time to tell her about my magic, or lack thereof, this was it. I opened my mouth but failed to summon the courage to do so.

"If you're preparing to step down, shouldn't Mom be doing things like this—leading more ceremonies?" I asked instead.

"Lyra does her fair share, but here is my concern, Adelaide. As I said, my seat as High Priestess and on the Court won't be the only one transitioning in the near future. At some point, Mathilde Augustine's seat will go to Dominic and then Gallad. Roman Bishop will likely die clutching his seat of power until someone pries it from his skeletal fingers, but even if he does move on in one way or another, his successors are all males."

"That would mean two High Priests of the Luna Coven," I murmured. That would be...unusual. Our people tended to be more goddess-oriented and matriarchal in nature.

"Exactly. Which means my line will be the only High Priestess. Your mother and I both agree that she is not the best person to balance out those masculine energies."

"And you think I am?" I asked with surprise. "If anything, my hellhound side only adds to it."

She nodded. "This is true, but we can work on developing your divine inner goddess, Adelaide. Look at your aunt Melaina. She's a hellhound, and I don't think anyone with eyes and a libido could deny that she's the embodiment of a goddess."

I snorted. The owner of Silk, the swanky nightclub, and my bio-father's sister was nothing less than sex and arousal in human form, and regardless of one's gender or preference, they'd die just for a chance to feel her body wrapped around theirs, her mouth on their flesh. She just had that kind of vibe.

"Aphrodite, no doubt," I muttered, and Saundra chuckled in agreement.

"I do believe this is why everything has come to pass as it has," she said. "Your growing role in leadership with SMA. Atanase leaving. Everything is aligning, Adelaide. This is your next chapter, if you choose to turn the page."

My brow lifted. "You're giving me a choice?"

"About your future? Of course. At least, to an extent. About Tuesday night's ceremony? No. I would like you there, whether or not you choose to lead it. But I do need to know ahead of time so we can prepare appropriately. Think about it and let me know as soon as you can."

Once again, I opened my mouth to reveal the secret I'd been keeping for a couple of weeks now—pretty much since I'd helped Sedona free Micah from the creepy angel doll. That was the last time my magic worked, and even then it hadn't been full force. It'd been dwindling more ever since, and I had no idea why.

Something within stopped me again, though. While she was probably the best person to offer help, she was also the last person I wanted to know. Besides, I was really hoping it was a temporary malfunction. Maybe I just needed to be turned off and unplugged for a while and take a break for myself.

As soon as I left the mansion, I felt like the weight of five Mount Mae's lifted off of me, and I drew in a long breath of clean mountain air. I'd not been feeling myself since Tase left, but being in that mansion with Saundra Beaumont scrutinizing me like she was had me completely out of sorts. Every muscle in my body was coiled in a ball of tension. Rather than jumping in my jeep right away and heading to the inn to see Michaela, I strode around the back of the estate and into the forest.

The sound of the waterfalls was muted this time of year. It wasn't quite frozen solid yet like it would be in a month or so, but it wasn't at its spring and summer rush either, when you could sometimes hear them from the center of town. The Beaumont property backed up to it, though, as did the estates of the other ruling families of the Luna Coven—the Bishops and the Augustines—giving us all direct access to the magic in the falls. So I could still hear them before I could see them through the bare branches of the trees.

Snow crunched under my feet, and I could smell more coming on the air. Another blizzard was being forecasted for later in the week, possibly Christmas Eve, just like last year. The reminder shot a pang through my heart. What was supposed to have been my best friend's wedding became a search-and-rescue party for a couple of human teenagers who'd gone missing in the storm. Tase had been the man I'd always believed in that day, the one others rarely saw, at least until he learned he was a father...and some other events that helped turn him around. Like the two of us finally admitting our truths to each other. I'd thought our on-again-off-again relationship had finally stayed in the on position for good since it'd been there for the last couple of years. Until now.

"Life's a bitch," I murmured, waving my hand to clear the snow from a fallen log on the edge of the drop-off that overlooked the falls. Of course, nothing happened. I couldn't even move a dusting of snow. "Fuck."

I plopped onto the log and bent over, pressing my forehead against my knees and letting my arms dangle, my fingers carving patterns into the snow. What was I going to do if my magic never came back? I didn't even know who I was without it. Just a hellhound? Apparently that magic remained, evidenced by the melting snow under my fingertips. I'd barely begun to embrace my father's side of me. My witch powers dominated. Well, truthfully, I let them. I favored them. I'd been a witch my whole life. I'd only been a hellhound for a few years. I didn't know how to be just a hellhound.

"What's wrong with me?" I groaned.

"Well, from here, the only thing I see wrong is you're missing one of these."

I looked up to see Rhian's thin form moving through the trees with two Coffee Haven to-go cups in her hands. She may have been a student at SMA, but she was so much more. As in, Rhiannon herself, a Celtic goddess of the moon. Still, she looked like a teen, as though she belonged in high school rather than college, let alone like a goddess. At least, in this form, with her waifish body, blue eyes that were too big for her fae-like face, and a pile of dirty blond dreadlocks wrapped with a scarf on top of her head.

"What are you doing here, and how did you find me?" I asked, accepting the cup she held out to me.

"I have my ways." She gave me a coy smile before gesturing at the empty space on the log next to me. "Do you mind? Or...you probably came out here to be alone, didn't you?"

"No, it's fine." I'd thought coming out here, so close to the falls, might give my magical energy a boost, but I'd felt nothing. I probably needed to dive in and swim in it, which I half considered. Even with the pond at the base nearly frozen over, I'd be fine. That was a benefit of being half-hellhound, I supposed. "How are you doing? Are you hanging around town for the holiday break?"

"I am. I love it here so much. And I'm really excited about the Luna Coven's Yule Ceremony."

I snorted. Of course they'd invited her—she was a goddess of the triple moon, of witches, after all.

"I've been there for the last two, and they have been so beautiful," she continued, her voice somewhat dreamy as she gazed at the falls. "Will you be coming? I know you don't usually, but I also know it's...different for you this year."

After setting my untouched coffee on the ground, my hand instinctively ran over the pile of bracelets on my other wrist, feeling the crystal energy zinging through my fingers. "Saundra wants me to lead it."

"Oh, I think that's a fantastic idea!" She paused, looking over at me. "But you don't, do you?"

I chuckled, but it fell flat, and suddenly tears sprang to my eyes. Fucking *tears*. I hated crying. I rarely ever did. But lately, they kept threatening at the most inopportune times.

"Addie, what's wrong?" Rhian asked, her voice softening as she ran a hand over my hair, and I realized it was the first human touch I'd had in…a long time. I couldn't remember the last time Michaela even hugged me or my mom—probably Thanksgiving. Now the tears overflowed, streaming down my cheeks faster than I could wipe them away. "I'm a good listener," Rhian whispered.

And for some reason, I gushed. She knew all about the truth with Tase—she'd been our source of information—but probably hadn't realized how much it hurt. And she knew nothing about my missing magic, not until now.

"I don't know what I'm going to do," I finally blubbered after laying it all out there. "No Tase. No teaching at SMA. No magic. Who the hell am I supposed to be now?"

Rhian's arm had slid over my shoulders, and she pulled me closer so my head rested on her narrow shoulder. "You're supposed to be Adelaide Larissa Beaumont, of course. Nothing more, nothing less."

"But I don't know who that is anymore."

"That's okay. From my many experiences over hundreds of lifetimes, I know that sometimes it can feel impossible to keep up with how much we change and evolve over the years. Life keeps whomping us with new experiences and situations so we can learn and grow. Just know you're exactly who you need to be at this moment. You'll figure out the next step in perfect time. And the one after that and the one after that."

"I wish I could feel so confident. I've never felt this *un*confident before, not even when I realized the boys would always fawn over Michaela and I would forever be the skinny, tom-boy best friend they'd always overlook."

"Psh." She gave a dismissive wave of her hand. "Boys are dumb. And that obviously didn't last forever. But it doesn't matter. Allow yourself to feel what you're feeling, knowing it's only temporary. You'll find your confidence again. And Saundra is right about your Saturn return. It makes everything feel so much worse. So…do you want to talk about the goddess energy? Because you have more than you think. Trust me—I would know."

Lifting my head from her shoulder and straightening up, I exhaled as I returned my gaze to the waterfall. "I know that as a witch, I'm supposed to embrace the goddess energy—and I do pay my tributes to her…you…them." Damn, it was weird talking about this with an actual goddess. "But did you hear what I just said? I've always been the tom-boy. I've never been the girly type. I'm not goddess material…which means I'm not really priestess material. No matter how hard Saundra Beaumont tries to make me be."

Rhian laughed. "Do you think *I'm* girly?"

I couldn't help but let out a quiet chuckle in return. Despite her petite size, with her dreadlocks and the all-black outfit of leather jacket, ripped-up jeans, and combat boots, she didn't exactly give off vibes of being dainty, soft, and tender. Yet…I could still feel her divine feminine energy. I also realized how similarly we were dressed.

"And you know I'm pretty badass when I want to be," she added, briefly revealing her true form—no longer the faerie-like waif, but a domineering goddess with well-defined muscles covered in bronze flesh, wearing the armor of a warrior, her expression fierce. Definitely badass, but feminine at the same time. She held it for a moment before reverting to her more normal college-student appearance. "Just like you can be. I can help if you want, not that I think you really need anything more than a reminder. You're going through a shit time right now, but you *will* get through this, Addie. You're one of the strongest women I have ever known, and that's saying a lot."

I heard the sincerity in her voice, which was humbling because that really *was* saying a lot. Not only was she a goddess herself, but she'd spent lifetimes in other realms with other goddesses and more here on this Earth with legendary leaders, possibly even Cleopatra herself. For some reason, her claim caused me to break down into more tears that would just not stop flowing. Every time I thought I was done, more poured out.

"What the hell happened?" Michaela's panicked voice rang through the forest, and with a whoosh of air, the moroi vampire suddenly stood in front of me, squatting so her greenish-gray gaze could take in my face. I could barely see hers through the tears. "Are you okay? What's going on? Why are you crying?"

Again I tried to stop, but instead I just flopped into her arms and let her hold me as I cried it all out. "I miss him so much, Kales. I just fucking miss him."

Michaela fell to her butt, holding me in her lap, and rocking me like a child. I'd never broken down quite like this before. This loss wrecked me more than I realized…more than I had wanted to admit.

"I'm so broken," I sobbed. "Completely and utterly broken. Shattered beyond repair."

Michaela sighed, smoothing her hand down my hair and back. "Oh, Bratty Addie, you are not beyond repair. I can't imagine what this feels like. I really don't want to. But you are Adelaide Beaumont. An extraordinary woman who cares so much more than she'll ever admit, but we all see it. If you didn't care, not only about Tase and Carter but about this town, it wouldn't hurt so much. The choice would have been easy, one way or the other."

I sniffled, nodding because she was right, but otherwise totally incapable of responding.

"This is your love pouring out, and it feels like it's breaking you, but in reality, it's strengthening you," she went on. "When you get beyond this—which you will, damn it—you will find your way to the best Addie Beaumont you can possibly be. And when you do, everyone who has put you and Tase and the rest of us in this position better watch the fuck out."

"Ain't that the truth," Rhian agreed.

I made a ridiculous, embarrassing sound as a laugh tangled up with my sobs. The air stuttered in my throat and chest as I inhaled deeply, followed by a long exhale, expelling whatever emotions remained. Finally, I swiped the tears from my face and fell out of Michaela's lap into the snow beside her.

"Damn. I don't know what came over me," I said after a few minutes of regaining my composure. "That was...intense."

"Do you feel better?" Michaela asked.

After taking a moment to self-assess, I nodded. "I do. Like a lot."

"You just needed to release," my mom said from behind us. We all looked over to where she walked the path that led from her house on the Beaumont estate. She sat in the snow beside me and pulled me into a hug. "You try to keep those feelings bottled up, baby girl, and at some point or another, they're eventually going to explode."

"I can't believe I cried like that, though. I don't remember the last time I did."

"It's better than exploding in other ways, especially as a hellhound endowed with your magical powers," she said.

I opened my mouth to come clean with the truth, but Rhian interrupted me. "Speaking of, Addie, why don't you make us a fire. It's getting a little chilly out here."

Indeed, the temperature had dropped as the sun lowered behind Miles Mountain. Rhian looked at me with a spark of the goddess within shining in her eyes. I didn't know what to make of it. Was she giving me a way to show my magic had left me without having to admit it out loud? Or did she know something I didn't?

The latter proved to be true when I flicked my hand and a pile of wood and twigs appeared. A swish of my fingers sparked a flame that grew to a nice fire.

"You really did just need to release," Rhian said with a knowing smile.

For the first time in nearly two months, a real grin graced my own lips.

❄

"I guess you're right, Mom," I said. "I did need that release."

Lyra laughed. "What was that? Did I hear you right?"

I smiled, leaning my head on her shoulder. "I'm so sorry I dumped on all of you, but I'm really grateful you were here. How did you all know where to find me, anyway?"

"Besides the facts that you were supposed to come to the inn and that I know all of your go-to places?" Michaela asked.

"Or that your jeep was still parked in Saundra's driveway?" Lyra added, and she shrugged. "I felt my daughter calling to me."

"I felt my best friend calling to me," Michaela said.

"I felt one of the most powerful witches I've ever met calling to me," Rhian finished, lifting her chin, and I almost burst into tears again, but a different kind. The kind that assured me everything would be okay.

"Oh, hey, this came." Michaela reached into her coat pocket, her hand fisted when she pulled it out. She pressed an object into my hand.

I didn't need to look to know what it was. I felt the

magic zinging through me. It was a figurine of Ganesha carved from amazonite, its calming, soothing, peaceful energy flowing through me as a reminder that I could overcome all obstacles. It was also the enchanted talisman I'd given Tase that was meant to serve as good luck for him and would create a portal home if he ran into trouble he couldn't escape. That it had come back to us meant he had found safety.

It also meant he was about to forget everything about Havenwood Falls, including me.

"They made it. They'll be okay," Michaela whispered, and I knew I just had to hang onto that belief.

And that I had to become the best Adelaide Larissa Beaumont I could possibly be. It was time to step and serve my purpose.

My heart pounded as I made my way through the snow to the ritual circle in the forest not far from where I'd sobbed my whole insides out two days ago. I didn't know why I was so nervous. I taught classes double the size of our coven. I'd led them all in battles against Zandra and other efforts to protect our town. Hell, I'd led half the town in those battles. But for some reason, a flock of starlings took flight in my belly, and my hands shook just enough that I thought I might drop the lapis lazuli ankh I carried. When Chewie trotted up to my side and Kylo Ren sauntered up to my other, followed by Skywalker dropping to my cloaked shoulder and Princess Leia flying just ahead, their magical energy infused me with a boost of confidence.

The coven members formed a large circle around an unlit bonfire, every one of them wearing a black cloak, their heads bowed so I couldn't see their faces from within their hoods as I passed around them. The magical energy crackled around and through us, powerful and empowering, billowing my own cloak behind me.

Taking my place on the small dais at the top of the circle, I looked out at all of them with their heads still bowed and felt the sacredness of the moment more than I had since I was a child. I bowed my own head for a moment in returned reverence.

"Blessed Yule, my sisters and brothers," I said, lifting my head and pulling back my hood.

"Blessed Yule," they all replied, looking up at me as they dropped their hoods.

My breath caught when I saw all of the familiar faces, and I forgot to be nervous, my heart swelling with unnamable emotions instead. I'd expected to see the elders—Saundra, Mathilde, Lyra, Patty Parker, Ronya Augustine, Roman Bishop, and others—but amongst them were the next generations, members who were more like me, usually doing ceremony by themselves or in smaller groups. Harlow and Taylor Augustine, Gallad Augustine, Curtis Parker, and others smiled back at me. All three Bishop brothers were in attendance for perhaps the first time ever. I could have sworn a twinkle of pride flashed in Roman's eyes before his usual look of annoyance overtook him once again.

I'd been denying and avoiding this moment for so long, but I realized now what Grandmother, Mom, and others had seen in me since I was young. Why they knew this would be my calling. Because leading this coven that protected my town, my people truly was my purpose. With each heartbeat, I could feel more power rising within me. I was meant to be here, serving them and our town.

I should have known, when I took a moment to look back, that the timing had been divine. I'd had to say goodbye to Tase and Carter at Samhain, not only the peak of Shadow Season but also the end of the Celtic year, when the Wheel of the Year turned to bring in a new cycle.

I wished I would have known then just how poignant this year's final holiday had been. If Saundra was right about a changing of the guard on the Court of the Sun and the Moon, we were coming to the end of an era…and the start of a new one, not just for me, but for all of Havenwood Falls. My being here, standing at the top of the Luna Coven's ritual circle, was proof.

From her place next to Taylor, Rhian gave me a small smile and a slight dip of her chin. A powerful energy surged up my spine, bringing goosebumps along my arms.

Everything really was about to change.

Swallowing, I rolled back my shoulders and lifted my chin, and then I began. "Tonight, on the longest night of the year, we come together to celebrate Yule. At Samhain, we honored endings and death. Now we welcome the new year as the light returns, and we embrace our new beginnings."

Blessed Yule from the Beaumonts and the Luna Coven

If you haven't met Addie Beaumont yet, you need to start from the beginning of Havenwood Falls with *Forget You Not* by Kristie Cook.

JOYFUL DESTINY

BY ROSE GARCIA

An Infiniti & Joe Christmas Story

Infiniti curled up on the window seat in the living room and stared out the glass. Snowflakes were falling from the December sky, the kind that were so big you could see the intricate pattern of columns and needles if one landed on your glove. Infiniti loved catching the flakes, and everything else about the wintry holidays, but something about this year felt different. And she knew exactly what it was. After Infiniti's mom had died in a house fire, she left Houston and said goodbye to her neighbor Jan, who was like a grandmother to her. Jan promised she would find Infiniti, but so far, she hadn't. Infiniti couldn't shake the feeling that something had happened to her. Something horrible. She thought the town peace ceremony last week would have helped ease her anxiety about it, but instead she felt as if the ceremony was having the opposite effect on her.

Was that even possible?

Pushing her melancholy thoughts aside, she closed her eyes and thought of the ceremony.

"Peace," she mumbled to herself, twirling the green amazonite bracelet around her thin wrist as she thought of Shaman Baba's words. "Peace. Peace. Peace." For good measure, like her witchy host Lyra Beaumont and her witchy best friend and roommate Taylor would say, she added, "Shanti, Shanti, Shanti."

A clanking of dishes pulled her away from her mantra as Lyra entered the room with a tray of teacups and saucers. She was a pretty woman with pale skin and short brown hair, with a build almost as small as Infiniti's. She often carried with her the scent of spicy fresh herbs, but as she walked into the room, the delicious aroma of fresh baked cookies followed her in.

Infiniti smiled. After two years, she was still so grateful that Lyra had taken her in. If Infiniti wasn't at the Sun & Moon Academy College, she was here. This was her home and would be until she finished college and could marry Joe.

"I hope I'm not interrupting you," Lyra announced.

Infiniti hopped off her perch and joined Lyra on the couch, glad for her company. "Nope, not at all."

"Good," Lyra said, handing Infiniti a delicate floral teacup.

Taking the fine china, she sipped the amber colored liquid. The spicy concoction slid down her throat, instantly warming her and making her feel a little better. "Mmm, delicious as ever. Thank you, Lyra."

"You are most welcome. But you know, the tea is even better with the cookies."

"You don't have to tell me twice," Infiniti said, eyeing the perfectly round light brown desserts. She took one then bit into it. It melted in her mouth with a sweet yet savory flavor, like a sugar cookie mixed with holiday spice. "Oh, wow. I think these might be your best batch yet."

Lyra was enjoying her own bite, too. "That good, huh?"

"Oh, yeah." Infiniti nodded. "That good."

The two continued sipping and munching, enjoying each other's silent company. But Infiniti knew what Lyra was up to. The wise witch had caught on to her mood and was offering her the comfort of food, drink, and a listening ear—all of which Infiniti wanted and needed.

But in true Lyra fashion, she was waiting for Infiniti to say something first.

After a final bite of cookie, Infiniti placed her teacup on the tray and sat back. She eyed the perfectly triangular shaped fir tree in the corner of the room. It dazzled with delicate ornaments of gold and silver that reflected the sparkling white lights that lined the branches. Gifts wrapped in matching silver and gold were stacked underneath. And even though the sight should have filled Infiniti with joy, it made her feel worse. Holidays were supposed to be filled with family, and despite having Joe and his parents and brother, and even Lyra and the rest of the Beaumonts, she had no real family in Havenwood Falls.

"Well," Infiniti blew out. "I guess you figured out I'm in a mood."

"I thought maybe something was up. Do you want to talk about it?"

Infiniti drew in a deep breath, trying to make sense of everything swirling in her brain, when her gaze landed on her amazonite bracelet. She touched the smooth stones. "You know how at the peace ceremony we wrote down our fears, or concerns, or even the names of loved ones on a slip of paper, and then threw the paper into the fire?"

"Yes, I know the ceremony."

"Well, I wrote down the name of my neighbor back in Houston, Jan, because I've been so worried about her. I thought that by doing that, I'd feel better. But I think I actually feel worse."

"I understand," Lyra said in her calming voice. "What is it you fear about her, Infiniti? What brings you the worry?"

Infiniti leaned her head against the couch cushion. "When I left Houston and came to Havenwood Falls with Joe, she said she'd come find me, but she hasn't. I can't help but think she's, I don't know, maybe…" Unable to verbalize her morbid thoughts, she let her words trail off.

"I see," Lyra half-whispered. She folded her hands on her lap. "You know, I believe everything happens for a reason, Infiniti. If Jan is meant to find you, she will. I have no doubt. Despite the time jump you experienced after arriving here, if it is meant to be, then it will be."

Sitting up with newfound hope, Infiniti smiled. "You think she could still show up? Do you think that's even possible?"

"Yes, and yes, anything is possible." Lyra took Infiniti's hand. "But the converse is also possible, that she is somewhere else and is destined to be there instead of here."

"Oh," Infiniti muttered, feeling silly and even a little selfish about making her own needs more important than Jan's. "I didn't even think about that."

She envisioned Jan in Houston, walking her dog, chatting with her neighbors. She might have even moved and retired somewhere nice. Like on a lake or beach.

Lyra patted her hand. "Don't feel bad about your feelings and your thoughts, Infiniti. Especially when they are good and true and rooted in love."

"I guess," Infiniti murmured, feeling defeated and not exactly knowing what to say anymore. Even if Jan was living her best life somewhere else, she really missed her and wanted her to come to Havenwood Falls.

Even if for a little while.

"Hey, I've got an idea," Lyra said, pulling Infiniti away from her thoughts. "If you don't have any plans this evening, how about we watch a movie?"

It was two days before Christmas Eve, and Joe was patrolling with his best friend Kase, a job he took with Sheriff

Rick over the holidays and summers. Taylor was busy with her family. That left her free, and a movie sounded like the perfect thing to get her mind off her worries.

"Yeah! I'm down for a movie. But...I need something first."

"Sure. What is it?"

Infiniti grinned. "More cookies."

The two spent the next hour chatting and laughing while baking another batch of cookies. And soon, the holiday cheer had returned, and Infiniti's sadness disappeared.

With a tray loaded with the fresh morsels and a hot batch of tea, the two settled in with blankets and pillows in front of the TV. And as Infiniti got swept away into the magic and beauty of the Polar Express, her favorite holiday movie from when she was little, she decided to believe that no matter what, things would work out.

She decided to believe in destiny.

A knock on the door the next morning awoke Infiniti. "Come in," she squeaked out in a sleepy voice.

Lyra cracked the door open and poked her head in. "I'm sorry to wake you, but I wanted to let you know that a blizzard is expected to blow in tomorrow. If you need to go into town for anything, you should do it right away. I'm headed in myself."

Infiniti had been through several hurricanes, some floods, a tornado, and her first blizzard last year. Another blizzard was probably no big deal, right? She sat up and rubbed the sleep from her eyes. "Um, should I be worried?"

"No, not at all. We'll have a lot of snow and some heavy winds, but we should be fine. We only need to be prepared to hunker down for a few days. So if you need anything from town, you should hurry in."

"Oh, okay. I'll text Joe. We were already planning to go into town today anyway."

"Very well. I'll see you later then."

"Okay. See you."

Flopping back down in bed, she rolled over for her phone and checked her text messages. As usual, being the early bird who never needed as much sleep as her, Joe had already texted at six in the morning. Glancing at the time, she saw it was nearly nine.

Joe: Hey, babe. Text when you're up

Me: I'm up!

A few minutes passed before he responded.

Joe: Babe, a blizzard is blowing in tomorrow. If we're still going into town, we should do it soon. Everyone is out preparing and getting last minute stuff

Me: Okay. Come get me in an hour

Joe: K. Love you

Me: Love you

After a hot shower, Infiniti slipped on jeans, a long-sleeved shirt, and a purple sweater. Then she dried her long, wavy brown hair. She was just starting to put on some makeup when the doorbell rang. She let out an *eep* and hurried to answer. Joe had been working the last several days, and she was eager to see her man.

When she opened the door, her heart skipped a beat. Joe looked amazing. He wore perfectly tight jeans and a snug long-sleeved black shirt that showcased his delicious muscles. As usual in the winter, he wore his blonde hair a little long, and a few strands hung in his blue-green eyes. But what struck her the most was the carnal wanting oozing from his intense stare.

"Hey, beautiful. Are you alone?"

She flashed him an innocent look, grabbing a lock of hair and twirling it around her finger. "Why, yes, I am. Lyra left not too long ago and should be gone for a while."

He licked his lips then stepped forward, wrapping his arms around her waist and planting his mouth on hers. They scooted into the house, and he closed the door behind him. His warm lips and velvety smooth tongue sent waves of longing pulsating all over her body.

"Can I have you right now?" he asked against her mouth, his kisses deep and hungry. "I really need you."

She threaded her fingers through his hair. "Only if you take your time with me."

He groaned. "I'll do whatever you want."

He lifted her up, and she wrapped her legs around his waist, their lips not breaking contact as he carried her to her room. With the lights turned low, they stripped off their clothes. And just like she wanted, Joe took his time pleasing her in every way imaginable.

When they were finished, they cuddled under the covers and Infiniti let out a contented sigh. "I will never grow tired of this."

He sprinkled her neck with kisses. "I know I won't."

She pulled back for a second, thinking about him being a wolf shifter. "Wait a minute. You won't as in you will never stop wanting me? Or you won't as in you never actually get tired?"

He smiled. "Both. I will always desire you as my one true mate, and I don't really get tired like that." He nibbled her ear. "If you want, I could go on and on and on pleasuring you."

She raised her eyebrows. "Really? And why haven't you told me this?"

He smiled. "I thought it was obvious." He climbed on top of her. "I can prove it if you want."

"Oh, I want!" She pulled him down and kissed him. "But not right now. I think something like that should wait until we are in our own place with no one to bother us for like days. Or weeks. That, and there's a blizzard coming."

He snuggled his head into the crook of her neck. "You're

right. We should get into town in case the weather turns sooner than expected."

With their clothes back on and the bed made, they left the house and headed to the town square. The area was packed with people scurrying about with armfuls of last-minute gifts. Joe rolled into the first parking spot he could find on the west side of the square.

"Where to first?" he asked.

She thought of all the gifts she had already bought—a new watch for Joe, a set of bath products for Joe's mom, a shaving kit for Joe's dad, plus a backpack for his little brother Boris. She also got a deck of fairy oracle cards for Taylor, with a matching manifestation calendar for the new year. She had already bought a necklace for Lyra, so all she needed was something for Saundra, Lyra's powerful and intimidating mom who sat on the Court of the Sun and the Moon, and something for Addie, Lyra's daughter, and one of the professors at the Sun & Moon Academy. She was sure to be seeing them over the holidays. At least, she hoped she would. She had no idea how long the blizzard would last.

She eyed the shops, noticing some of them looked closed. Luckily, she spotted people going in and out of Howe's Herbal Shoppe. "Oh, good, it's open."

Joe followed her line of sight. "Rose's place?"

She nodded. "Uh huh. I'm sure I can find what I need there."

Infiniti was bundled up in her coat, hat, scarf, and gloves, while Joe only wore a thin jacket. Hand in hand, they made their way to the shop and dashed in out of the snow. Warmth from inside engulfed them, as well as a cheerful holiday tune and the most calming and soothing herbal aroma.

The owner of the shop, Rose Howe, peeked at them from behind the counter. She wore her long red hair in a messy bun and was ringing up a customer. Next to her was Scarlet, Rose's daughter, who also went to SMA. She had hair that matched her mom's and was busily wrapping the customer's purchase.

"Hey, Fin! Hey, Joe!" Scarlet said with a smile.

"Hey, Scarlet!" Infiniti said, waving.

"I'll be with you two in a moment."

"No rush," Infiniti added.

The wooden shelves were lined with jars of twigs, roots, leaves, and powders. Infiniti drew in a deep breath, letting the pleasing scents work their way through her. Her mind took her to her first visit to Havenwood Falls. She had gone to the Cold Moon Ball with Joe, and then ended up in Rose's shop so the witch could help her get back to Houston. It was also where she and Joe exchanged their first kiss.

She looked up at him. "I really love this place."

He squeezed her hand, knowing exactly what she meant. "I do too."

The wall facing the picture window was arranged with holly and ivy and rows of hand-poured, holiday-scented herbal candles. Infiniti brought one to her nose and took a whiff, recognizing pine, vanilla, and maybe even a hint of berry.

"Wow," she said, passing it to Joe. "This is the one."

He breathed in. "It's nice."

She scooped up two candles, one for Saundra and one for Addie. Glancing around, she didn't think she needed anything else, so approached the counter. When the customer with Rose left, she set her stuff down.

"Ah, a great choice." Rose nodded with approval.

"Totally great," Scarlet chimed in. "When you light the wick, it crackles."

"Oooh, it does?" Infiniti asked.

"Yes," Rose replied. "I thought the crackle would add a nice wintry touch. Would you like these in gift bags with tissue?"

"That would be great. Thanks, Rose."

Rose took out two brown gift bags, and Scarlet started

rolling up the candles in red tissue. "Do you need any others? Maybe for any unexpected holiday visitors?" Scarlet asked.

With the impending blizzard, Infiniti didn't think she and Lyra would have any unexpected visitors. Unless, maybe, one of their neighbors popped in. She thought that might be a possibility.

"That's a great idea, Scarlet. Let me grab another one."

With the gifts paid for and ready to go, and after a quick goodbye, Infiniti and Joe headed back to the car. Joe cranked the engine and turned on the heat. Infiniti's teeth chattered from the cold.

"D-d-do you n-n-need anyth-th-thing?" she asked him.

He took off her gloves and rubbed her petite hands. "I'm all good. What about you? Do you need to go anywhere else?"

With the warmth from Joe's touch and the heater from the car, her body quickly stopped shivering. "The only other place I need to go to is Daily Knead. I want to get some cinnamon rolls and croissants." It occurred to her that she hadn't double checked that Joe was still off Christmas Eve. "Oh, you're still coming over Christmas Eve, right?"

"Yes, unless there's an emergency and Sheriff Kasun needs me," Joe said, pulling out of the parking spot and heading for Miller's Plaza, where the bakery was.

"He might need you?" A feeling of dread set in, and Infiniti was beginning to think he and Lyra were holding back on explaining the dangers of the impending blizzard.

"He might. In case there are any emergencies, the pack will be able to respond better than anyone else. Like last year's blizzard when we had to search for those two lost human teen boys. Remember?"

Infiniti nodded, the memory of that event coming back to her with a whoosh and making her stomach drop. "This morning I asked Lyra if I should be worried, and she said no."

"She's absolutely right. Even though it's a big weather

event, it's nothing we haven't seen before." He brought her hand to his lips and kissed her palm. "It will be fine."

When they got to Daily Knead, they found the place packed. "I guess everyone else had the same idea," Infiniti muttered.

"I guess so," Joe agreed.

They wiggled their way through the front door and patiently waited for their turn, their mouths watering from the smell of freshly baked bread. When their number was called, they were able to get everything they needed—a dozen cinnamon rolls, a dozen croissants, and since the blizzard was coming, they also got a dozen bagels. Plus, they got a couple of sandwiches for lunch.

"Well," Infiniti said with a smile. "At least we won't starve!"

Joe laughed. "Nope. We sure won't."

They found an empty table in the corner and sat knee to knee as they ate. With their bellies full, they went back to Lyra's. Infiniti set her gift bags under the tree as Joe's phone chimed. He pulled it out of his back pocket and read the message.

"My dad needs me to come home. Sheriff Kasun wants us to do some more patrolling. Apparently, the roads are getting bad already."

Her gut twisted tight while fresh worry that bordered on panic rushed her senses. "I don't like the sound of that."

He put his phone back in place, then tucked her long brown hair behind her ears. "I promise you, Infiniti, I will be fine."

"Okay," she muttered.

She eyed the gifts for Joe's family and Taylor. She had planned to deliver them Christmas Day but wasn't sure if she'd be able to because of the weather.

"What should I do about the gifts I was going to deliver on Christmas Day?"

Joe rubbed his chin. "I can take whatever you like to my family. I can also stop by Taylor's."

"Great idea. I have a big bag in my closet. I'll go get it really quick." With the bag in hand, Infiniti started filling it up. "Alrighty, that's everything."

Joe brought her in for a long, slow kiss. "I'll text you when I can, and please don't worry. Okay?"

She nodded. "I love you, Joseph Greg. Just be careful."

"I love you, Infiniti." He kissed her again. "And I will."

With Joe gone, Infiniti sat on the couch. Twirling her amazonite bracelet around her wrist, she admired the tree. It was so beautiful, probably the most beautiful tree she had ever seen—perfectly symmetrical and balanced, as if hand-crafted by the gods themselves. Even though Lyra had had the tree since Thanksgiving, the fresh pine scent still permeated the house. She raised a brow, wondering if some god had indeed fashioned the tree. Or maybe it was spelled. Considering her hostess was a witch, that was entirely in the realm of possibility.

Thinking of Lyra, she wanted to do something nice for her before she got home. She thought homemade tomato soup and grilled cheese sandwiches would hit the spot. She had a great soup recipe, and the pantry and fridge were stocked with everything she needed. Dialing up the Christmas spirit, she blared some holiday jams, singing along as she cooked, holding on to the idea that destiny would always take care of her…and Joe, too.

Infiniti awoke the morning of Christmas Eve with a chill in her bones. She sat up with a start. Had they lost power? She rubbed her eyes and studied her room. The light from the clock by her bed was still on, and the time was eight in the morning. She hopped out of bed and pulled open the drapes. A sea of blistering white swirled before her, and an eerie howl met her ears.

"Wow," she muttered. "I guess this is it."

She pulled the blanket from the foot of her bed and wrapped it around her shoulders. She reached for her phone to check her messages and saw that Joe had texted her an hour earlier. She scanned the message.

Joe: Babe. Looks like I won't be coming by today. The pack has been...

She clicked his name and called him without reading the rest, her heart beating out of control. He answered right away.

"Joe, is everything okay?"

"Yes, everything is fine. We've been called in to patrol the roads. The snowfall is crazy, and there are already reports of people stranded. We've got to get out there and help."

She calmed down, her mind grasping that when graduation rolled around in a year and a half, and after they married, this would be her life as the wife of someone who worked at the sheriff's department. And even though they'd already been through their fair share of life-or-death situations at SMA, and even before then when Joe had gone on a mission to find her in Houston, this somehow felt different. But even so, she needed to keep her cool.

"I'm so proud of you for helping people. Please be careful out there, and text me or call me when you can. I love you."

"I will. I love you."

With her phone held to her chest, she fell back on her pillow. It chimed, jarring her back up, but this time it was Taylor.

Taylor: Merry Christmas Eve!
Me: Merry Christmas Eve!
Taylor: Whoa, you're awake right now?

Me: Barely, lol My cold room woke me up

Taylor: Right? This weather is crazy! I wanted to text you early in case we lost signal later

Me: Good thinking

Taylor: I got your gift! It's under my tree. Can't wait to see what it is tomorrow. Did you get mine? I gave it to Joe

Me: Not yet. He's been called in to work. The pack is patrolling the roads. Not gonna lie, I'm a little freaked about him being out there

Taylor: Fin, he'll be fine. This is what he does. He can totally handle it

Me: I know. But still...

Taylor: I hear you. Well, I hope he can finish up sooner than later so he can be with you

Me: Same, girl

Taylor: I'll text you later. My mom is currently yelling for me #annoying

Me: Better go before she tells Santa on you lol

Taylor: lol

Infiniti rolled over on her side and snuggled into her soft pillows. She thought about going back to sleep but changed her mind. She didn't think she'd be able to even if she tried. Instead, she hopped out of bed, pulled on her plush purple robe, and slipped her feet into her happy face slippers.

A fire roared in the living room while the smell of nutmeg wafted from the kitchen. Infiniti followed the scent and found Lyra making a breakfast casserole. A potato hash sizzled on the stove, and a bowl of scrambled eggs sat nearby. The TV on the counter was turned on to a weather report and images of snowfall filled the screen.

"Well, good morning," Lyra said with surprised delight.

"Good morning," Infiniti replied, keeping her eyes glued on the TV as she poured herself a cup of coffee and added a heaping dollop of cinnamon creamer.

With the potatoes finished, Lyra started assembling her

dish for baking. "As you can see from the news, the blizzard is blowing in."

"I could tell. The house feels much colder than usual. That, and Joe texted to tell me that he and the pack have been called to duty, patrolling the roads.

With the casserole ready, Lyra loaded it into the oven. She washed her hands, freshened her coffee, and joined Infiniti at the table. "It's customary procedure for Sheriff Kasun and his staff to monitor the roads, nothing out of the ordinary." She took a sip from her mug. "The good thing, though, is the blizzard looks to be fast-moving."

"Yeah, that's what I told myself. I mean, not the fast-moving blizzard part, but the other part, that Joe out there patrolling is his job. And for me not to worry."

"I know it's easier said than done, but you are right, dear."

Infiniti sipped her coffee. "I also keep reminding myself about the destiny thing. That everything is going to work out the way it's supposed to. I mean, look at me! Joe saved me when I first came to Havenwood Falls. And when I left and my life was danger, he found me. Not to mention my latent time control abilities were awakened and I was admitted to SMA. I mean, if all that's not destiny, I don't know what is."

"Yours is quite a tale of destiny indeed," Lyra said with a smile. She considered Infiniti for a moment, then said, "You know, I am very proud of you. You have grown so much since you've been in Havenwood Falls."

"Thank you, Lyra," Infiniti said. "I feel like I've come a long way for sure."

The day crawled by, and Lyra and Infiniti prepped for Christmas Eve dinner as if a cascade of wind and torrent of snow weren't pounding the house. The turkey cooked in the oven, potatoes were peeled, and green beans were snapped.

They even fully set the table for six, just in case the snowfall slowed down enough for guests to somehow venture over.

Infiniti kept wondering if they'd lose power, but so far, they hadn't. It was as if the power grid of the whole town had been spelled to withstand a natural disaster. And maybe it had. She was about to get up from the couch and ask Lyra about it when a special report flashed across the TV—a bus filled with travelers had careened off the main highway near town, the same one she had crashed off so many years ago. It hung off the side of the mountain, and the only thing keeping it from plummeting was a thick pine tree.

Infiniti's gut twisted tight as her heart caught in her throat. Joe was out there. "Oh my god."

Lyra must've seen the report on the TV in the kitchen because she hurried into the living room. According to the reporter, with the visibility low and the highway packed with snow, it appeared the bus couldn't handle the curve of the road. Sirens sounded in the background as she went on to say that the nearby town of Montrose was sending in rescue crews and law enforcement.

"Wait a minute," Infiniti said to Lyra with a look of confusion painted on her face. "That's not us."

"It's not us because with the memory wards around town, no one even knows about us. But even though Montrose is near, we are still the closest ones to that highway, so I'm certain our people will be responding."

Fresh panic cascaded through Infiniti as she watched the scene unfold.

"He will be okay, Infiniti. They all will."

Even though Lyra's words were meant to reassure Infiniti, they didn't. The snow whipped around the highway like crazy, and the pine tree looked like it was ready to snap. If it did, the bus would dive, right along with whoever might be inside trying to help the passengers.

Infiniti shielded her eyes and turned away from the TV. "I can't watch."

Lyra went for the remote and turned off the broadcast. She faced Infiniti and placed her hands on her shoulders. "We don't have to watch it to know what's going to happen." Infiniti dropped her hands and studied Lyra as she went on. "Joe and the rest of the team are trained, not only under Sheriff Kasun, but also as students of SMA. They can handle this."

She let Lyra's words work her way through her before letting out a breath she'd been holding. "You are absolutely right. They will be fine. Every single one of them."

Lyra nodded, then redirected Infiniti. "Come on, I could use some help in the kitchen."

"Yeah, absolutely. Help in the kitchen. I can do that."

Between checking her phone for texts from Joe, exchanging texts with Taylor who kept reassuring Infiniti that everything would be fine, Infiniti and Lyra finished cooking the dinner and then finished cleaning up.

"Well," Lyra said after the kitchen was tidied up and the food was placed on warmers. "I'm going to freshen up before we eat. I suggest you do the same."

With an encouraging smile, Lyra headed for her room, leaving Infiniti alone in the kitchen. She stood there for a bit before going to her own room to get ready.

"He's fine," she muttered to herself. "Totally fine." She changed out of her leggings and into jeans and a sweater. "He can handle anything." She brushed her hair, then dabbed a little concealer under her eyes and applied some blush on her cheeks. "He's been through so much worse, so this is like, pfft, nothing."

Her phone rang, jarring her out of her self-talk. She grabbed it, saw Joe's face on the screen, and answered in a rush. "Joe!"

"Infiniti, I'm okay," he said quickly.

She lowered herself onto her bed, her hand pressing against her chest. "Oh, Joe. Thank God. I was so worried."

"I knew you would be. I'm so sorry, babe. But I was in wolf form and couldn't call you until now."

"I figured." Her breathing returned to normal. "So what happened? I couldn't watch the news anymore, and Taylor stopped giving me updates because it was just too much for me."

"We got everyone out of the bus safe and sound before it plummeted."

"Oh my god, what a miracle."

"You're not kidding." Infiniti heard some voices in the background and could tell Joe was distracted. "Babe, we've got a big truck here, and Sheriff Rick will be dropping me off over there in about an hour."

Her heart soared. "Really? Oh, Joe, I can't wait to see you!"

"Me too, babe. Me too. I'll see you soon. Love you."

"Love you."

Infiniti darted out of her room. "Joe is okay!" she called out into the hallway. "They all are!"

Lyra came out of her room with a big smile on her face. "I'm so glad to hear!"

"He'll be here in about an hour, too!" Infiniti added.

"And we will be ready!"

The doorbell rang almost to the minute. Infiniti flung it open, and Joe scooped her up in a hug. She held on tight, grasping him for a while, breathing in his fresh spicy scent. "I'm so glad you're here."

He squeezed. "I am too. But…I'm not alone."

He set her down, and she glanced behind him. "Who's with you?"

Out from the shadows emerged a tall figure bundled up in

a long dark coat, a scarf, a hat, and gloves. The only parts of the visitor that were visible were sparkling hazel eyes, rosy cheeks, a red nose, and a huge grin.

Infiniti gasped. "Jan!"

"My dear, Infiniti! Merry Christmas!"

Infiniti rushed over, stared at Jan for a moment in disbelief, then tackled her with a hug. Her heart swelled with unbridled joy as tears spilled from her yes. "It's you," she choked out. "It's really you."

They stood like that for a long while before they separated. "Yes, it's really me," Jan said between her own tears. "I finally made it."

"Why don't we catch up inside and get out of the cold," Joe suggested.

Once inside the warm house, Infiniti helped Jan take off her coat and accessories and hung her things on the hook by the door. "But how?" she asked Jan in disbelief. "How did you even..." Her voice trailed off. "You were on the bus," she muttered.

"Yes, my dear. I was on the bus heading for Montrose. Luckily for me, we ran off the road."

"That was lucky?"

"Yes, it was most definitely lucky. If I had made it to my destination, Joe would not have spotted me, and I would have never found you or Havenwood Falls. I've been searching for years, travelling from town to town."

Infiniti turned her attention to Joe. "You spotted her?"

"Yes, I spotted her in wolf form, recognized her right away from when I was in Houston. When I changed back to human form, and put on clothes of course, I went to her."

"And now I'm here. Finally," Jan smiled.

The doorbell rang. Lyra answered and in walked Addie. Lyra was all smiles, and a round of hugging ensued as group introductions were made.

"Well," Lyra announced. "We can catch up around a warm meal as dinner is ready!"

Arm in arm with Jan, Infiniti led her to the kitchen where everyone started serving up their plates. And as they gathered around the table and enjoyed delicious food, yummy drinks, and warm laugher, Infiniti's heart and soul overflowed with pure joyful contentment.

Destiny had taken care of her yet again, and just in time for a beautiful Christmas full of love and peace.

Merry Christmas from Infiniti & Joe

Read Infiniti & Joe's story by Rose Garcia in:
   Saving Infiniti
   Finding Infiniti
   Sun & Moon Academy Book One: Fall Semester
   Sun & Moon Academy Book Two: Spring Semester

THE GIFT OF FAMILY

BY E.J. FECHENDA

A McCabe Family Christmas Story

The sound of someone scraping their windshield outside breaking through his sleep, Mike McCabe parted an eyelid to read the time on the alarm clock. Pale light filtered in through the bedroom windows, and while seven in the morning was considered early for many, for Mike it meant he had slept in. Considering it was Christmas Eve day, he cut himself some slack and rolled over, his back to the clock, and his eyes landed hungrily on his mate. He and Anne had been married for decades, but one look at her creamy skin and the swell of her breasts made him feel like a teenager all over again. The house was quiet for now. In a few hours they wouldn't be empty nesters anymore and the rooms would be full of their family. With a predatory grin, Mike wrapped an arm around his wife and tugged her closer so she was flush against his naked body. Anne murmured something and blinked up sleepily at him, her green eyes soft and unfocused at first until she noticed he was wide awake and aroused.

"Let's take advantage before the kids get here," he whispered, then captured her lips in a sultry kiss. Before long it was no longer quiet as their moans filled the bedroom. Later, as they lay wrapped in each other's arms, while their heartbeats returned to normal, Mike started to tune into the noises around him again. He and Anne were mountain lion shifters and had heightened senses, so they could hear well beyond their property.

"Sounds like someone is shoveling," Anne murmured against Mike's chest, her breath tickling his hair.

"Yeah, and I hear a plow truck rumbling in the distance. I didn't think we were supposed to get snow until later this morning."

"That's what the forecast predicted." Anne sat up and stretched, a long and languid movement belying her feline nature that drew Mike's gaze to her breasts again. He was wondering if she'd be up for another round when the worry lacing her tone in her next statement made him reconsider. "I hope it doesn't delay the girls. The drive from Denver is long enough as it is."

He immediately thought of how treacherous the mountain roads could be when covered in precipitation. Rain, snow, or ice meant one small mistake could send a vehicle careening off a cliff. He rubbed a hand over his heart as anxiety began to creep in.

"They'll be fine." He tried to sound reassuring, but when Anne looked at him, he knew she saw right through him. He sat up too and reached for his phone that was on the bedside table in front of his alarm clock. "I'll call them to see if they hit the road yet." He climbed out of bed and made his way to the window that overlooked the street. Sure enough, at least three inches of fresh snow had already fallen and judging by the size of the flakes and metallic gray sky, the snowstorm had moved in early and was here to stay a while.

When he unlocked his cell phone to make the call, he

noticed a missed text message from their youngest daughter, Aster. It had been sent an hour earlier, letting them know they were on the road. He texted back, telling her about the weather and to be careful. Aster and her sister, Reeve, were driving together along with their mates and children. That was a whole lot of precious cargo, and Mike knew he wouldn't be able to relax until they got here. The drive from Denver to Havenwood Falls on a clear day was a good six hours. It was going to be a long day.

He joined Anne in the shower and let her know the kids were on their way. She nodded and took a deep breath. He wasn't an empath, but he sensed his wife's worry and distress through their mate bond. He knew she was thinking of their son Braden. This would be their fifth Christmas since he died, and it never got any easier.

"I know, my love, I miss him too, and the girls will be safe. Before you know it, our house will be so full of chaos, we'll be ready to kick everyone out." He hugged her close, pushing as much reassurance as he could through the bond. The hot water streamed over them as he massaged the small of her back. She softened against him, and he held her, letting her know that he would always be the rock she needed.

By the time they emerged from the shower, they were focused on all that still needed to be done. They hosted a Christmas Eve party every year, and that entailed a lot of work. Pushing his worries to the side, Mike focused on the "honey do" list Anne handed him. He had to fire up the smoker for the roast pig, which would take eight hours to cook. He had to make sure all of the exterior Christmas lights were working and chop extra firewood. Anne was going to be busy baking, wrapping presents, and getting last minute decorations up.

After a quick breakfast and coffee, they got to work, not stopping until lunch time. Mike cleared a path on the deck from the back door to the smoker, yet again, and propped the snow shovel against the house before stepping into the kitchen. The snow had been falling steadily all morning and accumulating fast. He took his wet boots off and joined Anne at the island where she was decorating sugar cookies.

"Smells amazing in here, honey," he said, placing a kiss on her cheek next to a dusting of flour.

"Almost done. Hungry? There's leftover lasagna from Napoli's in the fridge." At the mention of lasagna, Mike's stomach growled, and Anne chuckled. He pulled the container out and popped it into the microwave, grabbing two plates from the cabinet. Once heated, he placed healthy servings on each plate. Anne finished decorating just in time to eat.

"Any word from the girls?" Mike asked.

"No. Let's call them and see where they are."

Anne picked up the landline phone off the counter and dialed, putting it on speakerphone. After a few rings, Reeve's voice filled their ears, but it was just a recording for her voicemail. Next, Anne called Aster with the same result. Anne then tried Gage, Aster's mate, and then Patrick, Reeve's mate, and all of the calls went to voicemail. Mike frowned but shook it off.

"They're probably in a spotty signal area and will call soon," he said, and Anne nodded although he noticed the slight crease between her eyebrows. Leaning over, he pressed a kiss against that crease before standing up to clear their dirty plates from the counter.

Soon he was back to work clearing snow off the front walkway and driveway. It was almost a whiteout. He couldn't see any of the mountain peaks that surrounded the town. Even his neighbor's homes were shrouded in white, only a golden glow from interior lights visible in the blizzard, and the snow was coming down faster than he could shovel.

❄

An hour later, Mike entered the house through the attached garage and shook out his wool beanie that was crusted in ice. He left his soaked boots on the mat by the door in the mud room before walking into the kitchen. Anne was unloading the dishwasher and looked over her shoulder at him, her red hair swaying with the movement.

"Have you heard from them yet?" he asked.

"No and I tried calling again—still went straight to voicemail." Her face was pinched with worry, and he imagined he wore a similar expression. It was only a little bit after two in the afternoon and around the time they should have been arriving. Cell signal in the mountains was notoriously crappy, and the storm only made it worse.

"They'll be here soon," he said with forced confidence and poured himself a cup of coffee from the fresh pot that Anne had brewed.

From that point on they were both busy setting up the spread of food. He helped Anne carry trays overflowing with all sorts of deliciousness. Remy and Roxy arrived about an hour later. The twins they had adopted almost four years ago had finally settled into life in Havenwood Falls. With each year their traumatic past became more distant. Roxy was in her third year at the Sun & Moon Academy, where not only was she developing her tech skills, but had found her two mates. They filed in the door behind her, never far from her side. Roxy had opted to stay on campus over the winter break. Remy had recently been patched in as a member of the Sons of Infernal Night motorcycle club and had basically moved into the MC's clubhouse where he had a room. Mike shook his head and smiled when Remy dropped a bag of dirty laundry on the floor in the entryway.

"Nope—you know where that goes, mister!" Anne yelled across the room at him, not missing a thing. Remy flashed a devilish grin in her direction before hoisting the bag up over his broad shoulders and proceeded toward the laundry room, which was located by the kitchen.

Mike's parents, Daniel and Colleen, were the next to arrive, carrying in armloads of presents to stick under the tree.
"

"Are the girls here yet?" Daniel asked when he hugged Mike.

"Not yet. They should be here by now." Mike stepped out onto the front steps and peered through the heavily falling snow. All of the homes in his neighborhood were lit, and the way the light reflected on the snow made everything a hazy golden glow—fuzzy and dreamlike. His dad stepped beside him and placed a hand on his shoulder.

"They'll be here, son. The road conditions won't be the best. They're probably taking their time and being safe. Now, let's get inside. Your mom's making her famous eggnog."

With a final glance down the street, Mike followed his dad back into the warm house. A fire crackled in the living room fireplace, and the sounds of voices greeted him. While his dad wandered off to get a glass of rum-laced eggnog, Mike slipped into the quiet of his office and tried contacting his daughters again. All of his attempts went straight to voicemail. They were only two hours late. Two hours wasn't bad, considering the snowstorm. He tried to convince himself of this, but worry settled in his stomach like a cinder block. He and his wife had only gotten their daughters back two years ago, after being banished from the town for violating several supernatural laws. He couldn't bear the thought of losing them again.

"Grampa!" a voice called from the other side of the office door, followed by three impatient knocks. Mike grinned when he recognized his oldest grandson's voice. Jacob was Braden's only child. He quickly got up to open the door. As soon as the door was cracked, Jacob pushed it open and wrapped his arms around Mike's legs in a giant bear hug. Mike laughed and scooped up his grandson, noting that he had to strain more than usual. The seven-year-old had undergone yet another growth spurt. "Grandma said you need to bring the pig in. Can I help?"

"Sure thing, kiddo." Mike ruffled his grandson's auburn hair, causing it to stick straight up in some parts like little spikes. Jacob grabbed Mike's hand and tugged him out of the office, down the hallway, and into the crowded kitchen. Anne's aunts, Cordelia and Courtney, had arrived with their mates and were busy pouring glasses of wine. He greeted the twin sisters with a kiss on each cheek. Mike eagerly scanned the house, hoping to see the familiar red hair of his daughters, but couldn't find them. His eyes landed on Anne's face when she looked up from the stove. The worry lines seemed to have taken up permanent residence.

After slipping his boots on, Mike grabbed a giant platter that was on the kitchen counter before venturing out onto the deck to retrieve the pig, Jacob right on his heels.

"When are Aunt Aster and Aunt Reeve getting here?" he asked. "Uncle Gage and Uncle Patrick said they'd build a snowman with me if it snowed, and it's snowing!" He threw his arms out wide and spun in a circle as snowflakes fell around him.

Jacob was too little to assist Mike with the pig, but his chatter helped to distract him from his worry about the girls as he hoisted the pig onto the platter. Juices dripped down the sides from where the skin had cracked, and Jacob licked his lips.

"Better than bacon," Mike said and tore off a piece, handing it to his grandson, who eagerly snatched it from his hand and popped it in his mouth. Mike chuckled at the groan his grandson emitted as he smacked his lips. "Let's go, kiddo. You'll need to get the door for me."

As soon as Mike walked inside with the platter, practically every head turned in his direction, and noses lifted in the air as everyone caught a whiff of smoked meat, which called to their shifter nature. Remy's eye's flashed amber, taking on their cat shape, and his nostrils flared.

Then the landline started to ring, and Anne raced across the kitchen to answer. Her eyes widened with alarm, and seconds later the call ended.

"That was Audrey. Nicholas was called in to assist with a bad accident on the highway." She dropped that bomb before rushing out of the room. Mike quickly followed her into the den, where she turned on the news to catch the tail end of a special report about a commercial bus that had gone off the road and was basically clinging to the mountainside. Mike breathed out a sigh of relief because his girls weren't on a bus. The news droned on about the record snowfall, record wind gusts, zero visibility, and how the department of transportation was considering shutting down some of the highways.

Their family trickled out of the den as the news played in the background. Soon everyone was busy piling their plates with food, but Mike found his appetite had vanished. There wasn't room with the knot of worry taking up space in his stomach. Anne moved through the crowded dining room to stand by his side. For a few moments they stood watching their family enjoy themselves. The chorus of voices full of cheer, which was normal, expected, and should have lifted his mood.

"I'm really worried. They should have been here by now," Anne said as she blinked away a shimmer of tears from her green eyes.

Mike reached for her hand and laced his fingers with hers. "I know, baby. I'm tempted to call on one of the flying shifters to see if they can scout the road leading to town, but the storm is raging. I don't want to put anyone in harm's way, especially on Christmas Eve."

"Rusty or one of the other wolves that patrol the woods would have reported seeing their vehicle if they were in distress, right?"

"The sheriff's department plus the Kasun pack will be assisting with that accident. When's the last time you tried calling them?"

"Right before I joined you."

"Shit." He sighed and ran a hand through his hair, causing his dad to look at him with concern. Mike waved him off and released Anne's hand so he could walk into the living room. Just as he reached the front window to peer outside, there was a loud pop and suddenly his house, plus the entire neighborhood went dark.

There was a brief delay before the generator kicked in, restoring power to the house. One of the perks of owning a construction company was having access to top-of-the-line generators, Mike thought to himself. At least they didn't have to add sitting in a cold, dark house to the list of things to worry about.

He peered out the window again to see several of his neighbors had generators too, but several homes remained dark. Trees swayed in the howling wind that was driving the snow sideways. He hoped Aster and Reeve had decided to pull over somewhere and ride out the storm. Anne's reflection joined his in the window, and they remained there for quite some time, ignoring the sounds of the party carrying on behind them.

It didn't take long for their family to notice, and the living room was soon crowded as they joined in on the vigil. The sectional was full as well as the two leather chairs by the fireplace. Remy and Braden sat on the floor. Mike noticed Roxy and her mates were absent. They had at some point snuck off upstairs. If he listened closely he could hear their soft voices through the ceiling. At least it didn't sound like they were up to anything kinky. Thank you, Jesus, Gaia, plus all the gods and goddesses for that.

As the night wore on and the blizzard continued to rage without an end in sight, no one left. Everyone stayed to support Anne and Mike who had stopped trying to pretend they weren't freaking out. Anne's aunts set about cleaning up the food while Kaitlyn carried Jacob upstairs to put him to bed. He had curled up on the rug in front of the fireplace and passed out after the sugar high from way too many cookies and hot chocolate wore off. Nicholas, who was an EMT for the town, finally arrived with his very pregnant mate, Audrey. The bus accident had been cleared. He wasn't aware of any other accidents but promised to check in with the EMTs left on duty for any news. Mike's dad walked around the room with a bottle of bourbon, refilling glasses as they got empty. Conversations were carried on in hushed whispers as if everyone was anxiously waiting to hear a car pull in the driveway.

At some point Mike and Anne sunk down on the sofa. He put his arm around Anne's shoulders, and she curled up against his side, her head a comforting weight on his chest. The room quieted around him as people dozed off. His parents had retired to one of the guest rooms. He stared at the glowing embers of the fireplace, his eyes feeling weighed down by sand as he struggled to stay awake. It was after midnight when he was lulled to sleep by Anne's steady breathing.

The crunch of snow under tires jerked him awake, and he blinked at the sunlight pouring in through the window. A series of car doors slamming outside had him shaking Anne awake. She sat up and winced, rubbing at her neck.

"What's going on?" she asked, her voice husky with sleep.

"I think they're here!" He jumped up and ran to the front

door, ripping it open to see Aster and Reeve coming up the snow-covered walkway, each with a child on their hip and brilliant smiles on their tired faces.

Mike rushed outside to meet them with Anne right behind him. As soon as his girls were in his arms, it was like the cinder block that had taken up residence in his gut evaporated.

"Oompah!" Mina, Reeve's daughter, cried and wrapped her chubby arms around his neck, clinging to him. He breathed in her soft scent—baby shampoo with sweet undertones of vanilla.

"We were so worried!" Anne said when she hugged Aster.

"I know, and I'm sorry. The roads were terrible, and it took forever to get anywhere. We were less than one hundred miles away when we wound up getting stuck behind a four-car pile-up. Instead of waiting for emergency crews to clear it, we tried to take back roads to Burdorf Pass, but that was a mistake. Those roads were even worse. We didn't have any cell signal to let you know what was going on. Fortunately, by the time we backtracked to the highway, the road was clear. We should have just waited, but two fussy kids in the car makes for a long drive. We just wanted to get here already."

"What a nightmare. At least you're all safe. Here, let me take the little guy. Hi, baby boy!" Anne cooed at Egan, her two-year old grandson, who giggled in response when he was transferred from Aster's hip to his grandma's arms.

The commotion must have woken up everyone in the house because Mike's parents joined them next, his mom still in her flannel bathrobe.

"Come inside. It's freezing out!" She ushered the weary travelers inside. They experienced a bottleneck in the entryway, so Mike stepped into the living room to make space, spotting Aunt Courtney's husband, Brian, adding logs on top of the dying embers in the fireplace. Gage and Patrick followed him in, their arms full of bags.

"It's impossible to travel light when you have kids," Patrick commented.

"Wait until you have more," Mike said with a wink.

Patrick shook his head and sighed. "Did Reeve tell you already? We were going to wait until we got here."

"Tell me what?"

"So you don't know?"

"What don't I know?" Mike asked, thoroughly confused. Perhaps if he wasn't so exhausted and his brain was firing on more than one cylinder, he'd be able to follow the conversation.

"Never mind," Patrick said. "I'm going to put these away in the guest room." Before Mike could ask any more questions, his son-in-law was scurrying away.

"What was that about?" He turned to Gage, hoping his other son-in-law would enlighten him.

"Nope. I'm not getting involved," he answered with a nervous laugh. "I'd face the wrath of two redheads for any spoiler alerts, and even though I'm an alpha, the very idea makes my balls shrivel up in fear. You're just going to have to wait."

"Well, that is a good point. My daughters do have tempers." Mike decided to drop it and went to help get breakfast started, but he got as far as the kitchen entryway when Jacob ran up to him with Mina running on her chubby legs, doing her best to keep up with her oldest cousin.

"Grampa, we're supposed to be opening presents!" Jacob grabbed Mike's hand and proceeded to tug him back into the living room where the Christmas tree appeared to be perched on top of an avalanche of wrapped boxes and sparkly gift bags.

A harried looking Reeve rushed in. Her hair, usually styled and smooth, was pulled up in a messy ponytail, and her shirt had more wrinkles than an elephant's hide.

"There's my little escape artist," she said with a sigh of relief when she spotted Mina. "She was in the highchair eating breakfast, and I turned around for one second," she explained to Mike who just laughed.

"Aster used to do the same as she always had to follow you around. If you were done eating, then so was she."

Reeve's green eyes sparkled. "I remember how annoyed that would make me. She was like my shadow."

As if on cue, Aster and Gage's son, Egan, toddled in behind Mina. Oatmeal was smeared to the front of his Lion King bib, which was a gift given as a joke from Ryker Pride, an actual lion shifter. More oatmeal was caked to his pudgy cheeks. Aster rushed into the living room armed with a damp dish towel.

"I turned my back for one second," she started to explain, which caused Mike and Reeve to burst out laughing.

"Grampa, presents!" Jacob pleaded and tugged on the hem of Mike's shirt.

Mina copied on the other side. "Yeah, Oompah, pwesents!"

"Okay, fine," he conceded, pulling the ottoman closer to the tree so he could sit and hand out presents. "Girls, do you mind rounding up everyone else? And maybe round me up some coffee too? I'll keep an eye on these gremlins."

"Coffee," Aster said with a groan. "Too bad Coffee Haven isn't open because I could use three extra shots of energy tincture."

"You and me both, sister," Reeve said as she and Aster left the room.

Mike smiled at their retreating backs, an overwhelming sense of peace and joy washing over him. While everyone was exhausted after the long, stress-filled night, the storm had passed, and his family was safe. Where hours earlier his house was full of tension and worry, it was now a scene of happy chaos, how Christmas mornings should be.

His thoughts were interrupted when Nicholas and Audrey found him to say goodbye.

"Now that everyone is here, we're heading over to my parents for Christmas."

"Okay, and thanks again for staying last night and checking in with your fellow first responders."

"That's what family does. We might not be blood related, but I consider you an extension of my family. Didn't you know that when you adopted Roxy and Remy, we were part of the package?" Nicholas said with a laugh.

Truth was, long before they adopted Audrey's half-siblings, Nicholas was as close as a second son for Mike and Anne. Nick and Braden had been best friends and inseparable. Mike's throat grew tight, and he blinked to clear the tears that gathered in the corners of his tired eyes.

"Christ, I'm getting emotional in my old age. Come here, kid." Mike pulled Nick into a hug. "You are family and don't forget it. Especially when your little one arrives. We're here, always. Merry Christmas."

"Merry Christmas." Mike heard the same strain in Nick's voice and knew he was getting emotional too. Nick stepped away, and Mike opened his arms up to Audrey, who was heavily pregnant, giving her the choice to accept a hug or not. She had always been a little standoffish and not as touchy feely as other shifters, but she wasn't raised in an environment of love and support. Mike wasn't going to force physical contact on her either. Audrey surprised him by flashing a brilliant smile and stepping into his hug, which just filled Mike's heart to the brim. He gave up trying not to cry and let the happy tears fall.

Soon after Nicholas and Audrey left, the family members who remained filled every seat and vacant space on the floor in the living room. Mike had a steaming cup of coffee on the table next to him as he started to hand out presents.

Squeals of delight and joy along with the sound of wrapping paper being ripped, and the rustle of tissue paper, filled the room. Anne roamed around with her phone, taking as many pictures as possible to capture every moment. Mike knew her heart was as full as his as he felt that joy resonating through their bond.

When Mike paused handing out gifts to take a sip of coffee and steal a cookie off the platter Remy was hoarding, Gage stood up from where he was sitting on the floor. He held a present in one hand, the box topped with a giant green and gold bow. He cleared his throat and walked over to stand in front of Mike.

"You're not proposing are you, son?" Mike teased, which caused a ripple of laughter. Gage smirked and shook his head, handing the present over.

Mike untied the bow and carefully unwrapped the box. When he opened the lid and peeled back the layer of tissue paper, he sat in silence at the object nested inside: a sculpture no bigger than his hand made from a familiar blue-green stone. He lifted the statue out, marveling at the design. There were two mountain lions, one on each side of a divide in the stone. The mountain lion's tails were joined as if forming a bridge. The stone was cool to the touch and polished so smooth that it shone in the light.

"Is that amazonite?" Anne asked, moving forward for a closer look. She held out her wrist, displaying a bracelet made of the same blue green stones. The bracelet had been handed out to town residents when they attended the Magic of Peace Ceremony a few weeks earlier.

"It is," Gage replied. "The stone promotes peace, healing, and well-being. I had this made as a representation of the special relationship between our two dens."

Two years earlier, when Aster and Reeve's banishments were lifted, the Court of the Sun and the Moon had agreed to a pact of sorts between the Havenwood Falls mountain lion shifters, which Mike was the alpha of, and the Denver den where Gage was the alpha. With threats to the supernatural community increasing, the Court had decided that having open lines of communication and support with other supernatural groups outside of Havenwood Falls would be beneficial. Typically the town was protected by memory wards that made visitors forget their time spent in the magical town. Even residents who were gone longer than a lunar cycle lost their memories. The pact between the two dens bypassed this spell, allowing for Reeve and Aster, and their families, to return to Denver with their memories intact.

Two years later, Mike was still shocked that the Court had agreed to the arrangement, which was the first, and still the only, of its kind. He had a feeling it was a test, and if proven successful, more pacts with other supernatural communities outside Havenwood Falls would be established. Both Mike and Gage agreed to not abuse the privilege, and the statue further represented their commitment.

"Thank you. It's beautiful—very thoughtful," Mike said, rising to his feet so he could give his son-in-law a hug. After they broke apart, Mike placed the statue in the center of the mantle, a display of prominence.

He turned and met Anne's gaze. She smiled at him, her eyes shining with emotion. When he went to take his seat on the ottoman to finish handing out gifts, Reeve placed a hand on his arm, stopping him. He glanced down at her.

"Actually, Patrick and I have a present for you and Mom. We didn't put it under the tree."

"Oh?" One of Anne's eyebrows rose in question when she accepted the present Reeve handed her. With her long, graceful fingers, she peeled the wrapping paper, revealing the back of a frame. When she flipped the frame over, she gasped, and her head whipped up, her eyes seeking out Reeve. "Really?" She practically squealed and shoved the frame into Mike's hands so she could hug Reeve.

Mike glanced down at the frame, curious as to what elicited such a reaction, and his heart practically stuttered when he took in the black and white ultrasound image of his next grandchild. Now the conversation he had with Patrick earlier made sense.

"We're going to be great grandparents again?" Mike's mom cried out when he passed the frame to her. Tears filled her eyes, and soon the whole room was congratulating the expecting couple. Well, except for the other grandkids. They were too absorbed in their new toys to pay any attention to the adults.

Mike stepped back to watch everyone, to witness the love and happiness in the room. How Patrick stood next to Reeve, his hand protectively rubbing her belly, when Roxy and her mates offered their congratulations. Gage and Aster were talking animatedly with Aunt Courtney and Aunt Cordelia while their mates, Paul and Brian, started pouring champagne in celebration of the good news. Remy helped by passing glasses around. Kaitlyn and Anne studied the ultrasound image again, trying to see if they could determine the sex.

Mike's dad came up to him and placed a hand on his shoulder, giving it a light squeeze. "Feels good, doesn't it, son?" He tapped his champagne flute against Mike's.

"Yeah. It really does." It felt more than good. Not only was his entire family together again, but his family was safe and growing. For the first time in a long time, Mike experienced a deep sense of peace and hope for the future.

Merry Christmas from the McCabe Family to Yours

Have you read all of the McCabe family books from E.J. Fechenda?

Fate, Love & Loyalty
Forever Loyal
Fated Beginnings

A PROMISE FOR THE NEW YEAR

BY E.J. FECHENDA & ROSE GARCIA

A Cat & D New Year's Story

DINGANE

*I*f someone told me five years ago that I'd be standing on top of a ski slope, getting ready to plummet down the side of a mountain at breakneck speed with a gorgeous girl by my side, I would have never believed them and would have curled inward at the cruelty of such a suggestion. I like to think I'm a different person now, and I am. Five years ago, I had no free will. Five years ago, I was surrounded by darkness and forced to carry out atrocities that haunt my nightmares.

For my kind, an Impundulu lightning bird, servitude in the form of a familiar to a mage who practices the dark arts is the usual fate. But five years ago, my fate changed and here I am, halfway around the world from my homeland of South Africa. There are moments, like this one, where I'm convinced it's all a dream and I'll wake up shackled and a shell of the man I've become. As if sensing my thoughts, Cat Vega reaches over and squeezes my gloved hands with hers.

"Ready?" she yells over the whine of the wind that whistles across the top of the peak. I nod and pull my goggles down from where they're perched on the top of my head. Cat counts down from three and launches down the steep mountainside. I give her a few seconds' lead time before barreling down after her. I had never skied before moving to Colorado, and it took me a few runs to get used to the sport. Now, despite the cold, I can't get enough of it.

Skiing is freeing and provides the same exhilarating rush as flying.

When I'm in my lightning bird form, I can soar above the land for hours. Skiing is akin to that sensation—soaring high up where the air is clearer, and I can race into the wind. Before, when I was tied to that mage, she controlled my every move. Flying wasn't an escape like it is now. Back when I was forced to shift into my lightning bird form, that meant I was about to become a harbinger of death and destruction. No matter how hard I tried to fight it, the mage always won and would cackle in delight when I struggled. She punished me with cruelty, over and over. Most of my wounds on my dark skin have healed, but the psychological scars remain.

Then the mage died without leaving an heir to inherit me, and my curse was broken. I had no home except for the prison I was eager to leave behind, so I wandered. The nomadic lifestyle suited me. I traveled from village to village until I made it to the city of Johannesburg. There, I was merely an ant in a colony and was able to get lost in the large population. For two years I lived anonymously. I used my youth and strong body to learn a trade and worked in a factory that manufactured components for electric vehicles. One moment I was the average worker, and the next, the factory exploded and collapsed into a pile of flaming rubble.

I was inside when it happened, and on instinct, I shifted. My wings formed a shield, like an umbrella, that protected me from the fire, the one thing that can end my immortal life, and falling debris. As I soared upwards and free of the disaster, the anguished cries of my co-workers reached me. Cries so similar to those from my past that I had caused. They couldn't be ignored, so I swooped down, despite the risk the flames posed, and used my enhanced vision to detect survivors. I proceeded to rescue as many as possible. Many of the survivors were bleeding, which called to my thirst for blood, but somehow the need to help overrode that thirst.

By the end, I had saved over twenty people, and my presence made more headlines than the catastrophe itself. With my huge wings and the lightning that arced from my body, I was considered an angel. A miracle. A savior. I knew, deep down, I was no such thing. But outing myself so publicly did work in my favor, or perhaps it was fate intervening again. A recruiter for a new college that was opening, the Sun & Moon Academy College for Supernatural Guardians, or SMA, saw a video clip of my rescue efforts online and tracked me down. So here I am, halfway through my third year at the academy, with a girl I don't deserve racing ahead of me. Her laugh trails behind in her wake, and I will chase that laugh for centuries if she lets me. That's the kind of light I need in my life.

"*¡D, apúrate!*" she hollers in a taunting tone.

I do as she commands and bend at my knees, tuck in my arms, and lean forward. The new position works, and I start gaining on her. She peers over her shoulder, her dark hair whipping around her face, and she whoops when she sees me moving closer. This makes me grin. The cold causes my teeth to ache, but I keep smiling all the way down the mountain. Cat reaches the bottom first, just barely, and I come to a stop beside her, kicking up a wave of snow with my skis. She throws her arms around me, and I catch us both before we fall backwards. Then she's kissing me, and everything around me fades. The memories of my past and the journey to get to this moment are forgotten the second her lips are pressed to mine. Cat is a balm for my tortured soul.

After a few more passes on the slopes and lunch at Burger Bar, we head back to NamaStays Inn, where we have a cabin for the night so we can celebrate New Year's Eve in town. It's a welcome break from the campus under the mountain where we're both staying over the holidays. Fin and Joe, who go to school at SMA too, are meeting us in the courtyard for pre-dinner drinks. We quickly shower, dress, and head out to meet our friends. Once again, I'm bundled up in flannel lined jeans and a thick winter coat. While I have been living in Colorado for three years now, I don't think I'll ever get used to the cold. Cat, however, seems to love it. She's wearing her usual black leather pants with a low-cut, long-sleeved purple top that shows off her amazing body. I'm already looking forward to staying warm with her under the covers tonight.

The inn's courtyard is an enclosed outdoor stone patio replete with a fire pit and full-service bar. The patio is similar to the one at the winery, but on a smaller, more intimate scale. Cat takes a spot closest to the fire on a chaise lounge built for two. I slide in behind her and wrap my arms around her slim waist, pulling her against my body. She looks over her shoulder at me with her full lips curled up in a dreamy smile. Without hesitation, I lean forward and give her a kiss just as Infiniti joins with drinks in hand. Joe has a work thing, but will be joining us later.

Sipping on the Irish Whiskey-laced hot cocoa, I hold Cat while she and Fin chat about dinner plans, but soon I'm zoning out and focusing on the rings that are practically burning a hole in my pocket. There's one more errand to run, and I have a little over an hour, so it should be easy to slip away real quick. The hard part, though, will be later when I actually give it to her. A bead of sweat forms on my temple despite the cold as I envision giving the ring to Cat.

I'm not asking her to marry me. Our relationship isn't nearly on the same level as Fin and Joe's, but the rings aren't insignificant either. I just hope Cat doesn't freak out. I mean, our relationship started as a hook-up of convenience during one of the many challenges that are part of SMA's curriculum. Plus, I'm not the only one with issues. It has taken a long time for Cat to let her walls down around me, and it has taken me a while to share my insecurities with her—the fear that I am tainted by darkness—that there's permanent residue on my soul left behind by the mage who held me prisoner.

Once again, as if sensing my inner turmoil, Cat places a hand on top of mine and threads our fingers together. She relaxes back against me, and I run my nose along her neck, breathing in the spicy clove scent of her perfume that clings to her silky tan skin and the rich iron of her blood that pulses beneath, which in turn relaxes me. She's like my personal form of aromatherapy. This connection helps to dispel my uncertainties over the rings, yet some doubt lingers. Come midnight, I'll know if Cat is into me as much as I'm into her. I hope I'm not about ready to fuck everything up.

CAT

When I was little, even though I wasn't supposed to show anyone what I could do, I dreamed of using my abilities to help people. I'd spend weekends on my bike, patrolling my neighborhood, waiting to find a neighbor in danger. Sometimes I tied a sheet around my neck, letting it blow behind me like a magnificent cape. But when I was fifteen, my family was murdered by the deadliest transhuman alive—Tavion. That's when everything changed for me. He spared my life, but kept me as his pet, forcing me to hunt and kill for him. Sometimes he'd want me to kill other transhumans, but mostly he wanted me to kill regular humans. He hated humans and blamed them for ruining the world. In his mind, the planet was better off with supes only.

I did his bidding for years all while plotting a way to escape his clutches. As luck would have it, he became obsessed with a girl named Dominique. He feared she had the ability to end him. I hoped he was right about that, but I didn't stick around to find out. Instead, when he left on a mission to track her, I made a run for it. For years, I darted across the globe, believing that moving around would make me hard to find. I spent time in New York, Costa Rica, then Spain, until I eventually found myself back in the United States, in sunny Florida.

But fate didn't want me to stay hidden.

One night, my run-down motel caught on fire. I zoomed in and out of the building with sleeping guests, not even realizing my actions were being recorded on a phone across the street. The footage ended up online. Over a million views later, I was tracked down in California by a recruiter saying he worked for a college called SMA. I never thought I'd end up at college. Let alone a college for students like me. With a guy as magnificent as Dingane.

Tall and muscular with gorgeous skin as dark as night, intense brown eyes, and seductive full lips, I can't believe he's mine. The mere sight of him lights a spark of desire deep inside of me, and when he slides behind me on the chaise lounge as I'm chatting with Fin, it's all I can do to keep from pouncing on him. Instead, I calm myself and thread my fingers through his, trying to keep my cool as Fin and I chat about dinner plans. But then he runs his nose along the back of my neck. A cascade of shivers erupts all over my body, in anticipation of D biting me. He just places a gentle kiss instead, and I'm swept away by the mere thought of what we'll be doing to each other later that night.

"Um, y'all need some alone time right now?" Infiniti asks.

Her head is tilted, and she's flashing me a sheepish grin.

Her question brings me back to our conversation, and I clear my throat. "Sorry, Fin. I didn't catch that last part."

She laughs, then shakes her head a little, as if knowing exactly where my thoughts had wandered. "So, dinner? Fallview Tavern and Grille? It sits at the top of the falls, and it's supposed to be awesome."

"Sure," I say. "That sounds great."

"D," she says, leaning over to catch his attention. "You okay with that?"

"Um, yeah, whatever you two want is fine with me."

"Perfect!" She pulls out her phone and starts clicking. "Hey, they've got a table open at eight." She clicks some more, then lowers her phone with a smile. "We are all set for dinner for four at eight o'clock."

D gets up from where he's nestled behind me, and I turn to face him. A look has come across his face, like worried concentration. It's a look I know all too well from my past. He's hiding something. I thought back to a couple of weeks ago, back in the dorms when he had received a call and said it was his roommate Clay when it clearly wasn't Clay. He had never said who had truly called, but his face held the same expression as now.

He is up to something.

"Ladies," he announces. "If you two don't mind, I'll leave the remainder of the plans in your capable hands while I run a quick errand." Without giving me a chance to respond, he kisses me on the lips. "I'll be back soon."

"Oh," I mutter. "Okay."

I've been letting my guard down with D, as he is with me, though I still keep plenty of secrets to myself. I'm sure he does too. I can't help but think he's left because of one of those secrets. Especially since things never seem to work out for me.

"Hey," Fin says, pulling me from my thoughts. "He's just going to run an errand."

D and I had spent a glorious morning skiing, and now he's running off somewhere. I'm sure Joe wouldn't have done that to Fin. Her life is perfect. I cross my arms in front of me. "I have bad luck with guys, so having one take off out of the blue to run an errand he hadn't mentioned before does not sit well with me. Plus, he lied to me two weeks ago about a phone call he got."

"He lied?" Fin scrunches up her pretty little face, thinking for a few seconds. "That doesn't sound like D."

Flipping my hair with my hand, trying to convince myself that D didn't matter to me, I say, "Men are dogs. So maybe the D you and I think we know isn't the real him."

Fin rubs her head. "Listen, let's not jump to any conclusions, okay? You can talk to D later when y'all are alone."

I shrug my shoulders, playing the role of cold hard bitch I'd been forced to play for so many years, a role that protects my heart from pain and suffering. I'm falling hard for D, but maybe he isn't falling hard for me.

A look of perpetual optimism comes across Fin's face. "Well, Joe is working right now, and dinner isn't for another two hours. Why don't we run some errands of our own? I'm sure there are tons of shops having after-Christmas sales. What do you say?" And then she adds, "Might do you some good. Plus, I really think whatever D is doing is perfectly innocent. The guy is totally into you."

Shopping is my least favorite activity, but Fin is right. Doing something with her would get my mind off whatever D is up to. "Fine, I agree. Let's go before I change my mind."

Fin is probably my closest friend at school. We've had our fair share of fights and arguments, especially when I went after Joe during the first semester of our freshman year, but through it all we have learned a lot about ourselves and each other. She is my polar opposite in every way, which is why I think our friendship works.

"Hey, Fin," I say, as we walk to the NamaStay Inn shuttle that drives people back and forth from the town square. "Thanks for being such a great friend."

She smiles and wraps her petite arm around my waist. "Ah, Cat! That's the nicest thing you've ever said to me."

With a small smile and a raised brow, I tack on, "Don't get used to it."

Heading into town, I tell myself D is just another guy. That he isn't important enough to hurt me. That I am tough and don't need anybody.

I just wish I could believe myself.

DINGANE

Shit. I'm already screwing things up. The shadow of distrust that passes across Cat's eyes when I leave her and Fin at the inn kills me. All I'm doing is picking up a bouquet of flowers to surprise her from Fairy Tale Florists, but now I'm thinking that was a dumbass move. I honestly don't know what I'm doing. This is my first relationship and to have met someone with a past so similar to mine? Someone who understands my demons? I mean, we were both recruited because our abilities were recorded, when we were both rescuing people from burning buildings, and the videos went viral. What are the odds? Our connection is rare, and I can't lose her.

My secrecy over the rings has already resulted in one giant fight. It happened shortly after the Magic of Peace Ceremony that was held in Havenwood Falls a few weeks ago. That's where I got the inspiration for the rings. Prayer beads, or malas, made of amazonite were handed out to everyone. I overheard someone say that amazonite is also known as the Hope Stone and that the bluish green stone has healing properties, especially for emotional, mental, and spiritual well-being, like for those who suffer from past trauma. After further research, I learned the stone can help align your heart chakra. At the thought, I run a hand over my chest, subconsciously rubbing the X-shaped scar that mars the skin over my heart. The only mark left behind by that evil mage.

Knowing Cat and I share past trauma and are in search of finding inner peace, I decided to have matching rings made out of amazonite, but I wanted it to be a surprise. The next day after the peace ceremony, Cat and I were back on campus, and I couldn't stop thinking about the rings. I was a man on a mission, and it seemed like Cat was on her own mission to spend every second with me. Normally, I wouldn't mind, but I needed time away to sneak back into Havenwood Falls. Fortunately, my roommate and best friend, Clay, was happy to help me with my plan, and so we told our girlfriends we needed guy time to shop for Christmas gifts.

I went to Summit Jewelers, the only jewelry store in town, and explained to them what I was envisioning—matching bands made of resin that have Rocky Mountain Juniper encased inside along with chunks of amazonite. The juniper represents growth. Both the juniper and the amazonite are native to Colorado, which is where Cat and I met.

Once I placed the order, practically draining my meager savings to pay for the rings, Clay and I returned to campus. Cat noticed I had come back empty-handed, but at least Clay had a couple of bags, so it didn't look too suspicious. But when the manager of Summit Jewelers called with an update that the rings wouldn't be ready in time for Christmas and that I'd have to wait until closer to New Year's, I ended up whispering into the phone and leaving the room. She was narrowed-eyed and suspicious, as she should have been. After I had finished the call, I ended up lying and said that Clay had called, but as soon as the lame explanation spilled out of my mouth, Clay walked into the room.

Cat lashed out at me with some choice Spanish phrases, then stormed out of the room. The death glare she had directed at me nearly cut me in two and left me feeling hollowed out. I received the silent treatment for the longest twenty-four hours of my life. I'm not above groveling, and it took some major convincing (and a promise of unlimited foot massages) to get back into Cat's good graces again. She can't resist my foot massages. They're her kryptonite. Hey, every superhero has a weakness.

So here I am feeling like shit as I head into town because I know I'm hurting the woman I'm falling in love with. I want everything to go as planned and only have a few hours left. I nervously pat my pocket again to make sure the rings are still there.

When I get back to the inn, Cat isn't there. I glance around to make sure her stuff is still in the cabin, and luckily it is. I'm about to sit on the chair in the corner to wait, when she opens the door, sending a breeze of cold air into the room.

I shoot up to my feet with an apologetic smile and hand her the vase bursting with white lilies—her favorite flower. "I went into town for these. I wanted to surprise you."

She sets her stuff on the table, her expression looking happy to see my offering, but also still a little hurt.

Setting the vase on the table, I say, "Cat, babe." I reach out for her fingers and tug her to me. "Please don't be mad at me."

Her fiery Latina sexiness returns as she slams her hands on my chest and pushes me onto my back on the bed. She jumps on me and straddles me with her strong legs. "Prove yourself to me and maybe I won't be mad anymore."

I sit up and run my hands up her back and into her hair. "I'll do whatever you want, kitty cat," I say teasingly before I kiss her.

The kiss leads to us being late for dinner, but that's okay as we emerge from our room blissed out and conflict free. We meet our friends in front of the inn where Jakeel, our Luber driver, is waiting in his older model orange hearse. Fin makes a joke that I have heart emojis for eyes, which makes Joe snort.

Throughout dinner I'm distracted and suddenly nervous about the rings. Cat and I have been so up and down lately, all because of my being secretive about the damn jewelry in the first place. So far, they were having the opposite effect of what I intended. Does Cat not trust me? Will she always think the worst? One glance across the candlelit table to Cat helps to silence those doubts. She gives me a small, playful smile before raising her glass of sparkling water to her lips, which are still slightly swollen from earlier. I smile back and nudge my foot against hers under the table.

So far, everything is going great. I just hope it stays that way.

CAT

I had been so worked up when D left me and Fin at the firepit, I had been ready to call it off with him, pack up my stuff, and leave the inn. But when I return and walk into our cabin to see him with flowers, I melt. I've never had a guy give me flowers before. And the way he asks for my forgiveness and the lovesick look on his face has me wanting him like I've never wanted anyone. So I have to do what I have to do. I pounce on him.

Having my way with his magnificent body is so worth being late to dinner. But as we near the end of our meal, he starts acting strange again. He drops his napkin on the floor, fidgets with his silverware, and bounces his leg under the table. My gut twists into a giant knot. Is he going to break up with me? Did he want one last rendezvous with me before cutting it off? Is that what this is all about? I recall an article I read about breakups coinciding with major holidays.

Eyeing Fin and Joe, I see how their bodies angle toward each other as if drawn together like magnets. Joe can't keep his eyes off her, or his hands. He is stroking her arm lovingly, and I don't even think he knows what he's doing. He's just so into her.

Glancing at D, I wonder why I can't have something like that. Why is everything so hard for me? I crumple up my napkin and toss it onto my plate as I rise to my feet. "Excuse me."

Fin rises to her feet. "Me too!"

She trails behind me as I weave my way around the tables to the back of the restaurant where the restrooms are located. Once inside, she plants her hands on her petite hips. "Um, what is going on? One minute you and D look like you're in love. The next minute, you look like y'all don't even want to be in the same room. I thought he gave you flowers and everything was better? And you guys, you know, kissed and made up."

My mind is calculating how to avoid being a victim when an idea comes to me. "Well," I announce to Fin, "I'm going to break up with him tonight."

Her mouth falls open. "Uh...what?"

I take my red lipstick out of the small black purse slung across my black sequined leather bodysuit I'd been saving for this night and lean toward the mirror, feeling a little bit better to be in control of the situation.

"Yep," I say, following my full lips with the red color. "I'm doing it after we ring in the new year. Happy New Year, I'm done with you."

Infiniti blinks, but doesn't say anything. "Um, hold that thought. I gotta pee."

She slips into a stall while I reach for my boobs and give them a lift, accentuating my already full display of cleavage. Then I thread my fingers through my long dark locks.

Admiring myself in the mirror I say, "Better for me to end it than him. Strike hard, strike fast."

When she finishes, Fin comes out of the stall and washes her hands. "I support you one thousand percent, Cat. So if you think it's best, then I'm with you."

"Thanks, Fin. And yes, it's absolutely for the best."

Back at the table, Joe and D are chatting about football, but stop and rise to their feet when they see us. Joe smiles at Fin, and D, well, he looks a little pained. Not that it matters anymore. After I break up with D, I'll move on. *Adiós, pendejo.*

Back in our Luber and heading for Mount Mae Ski Resort where the fireworks display will be, the air in our small party of four has definitely changed. Joe thrums his fingers on his knee, Infiniti nervously wraps one of hers around a strand of long brown hair, and D looks a million miles away. My mind drifts too, thinking of how D and I went from friends to lovers during our school task force challenge when Fin and I had gone all "Freaky Friday" and switched bodies. That was the second semester of our freshman year, and we have been together ever since. I told him so much about myself, more than I had ever told anyone. Suddenly, I regret sharing so much with him. Not just my body, but my heart and even my soul. Serves me right for letting my guard down and trusting him.

The Luber driver pulls up as close to the resort as possible and drops us off. A band is on a stage, rocking out, and bodies are dancing and partying at the base of the blue square slope. The frigid air feels good against my skin, but I can tell D is bracing himself against it. His broad shoulders curl in a little as he pulls his coat tight around him. Joe and Fin are so close, it's hard to tell where she ends and he begins.

"Let's move closer to the stage," Fin prods.

They lead the way through the crowd, going as far as they can until the four of us are shoulder to shoulder with the rest of the spectators. D wraps his arms around me from behind and snuggles me to him. I stay in his embrace, letting myself enjoy his company until the last minute.

The band finishes their song, and Mayor Barbie Stuart takes over the mic. She welcomes the crowd, says a word about the significance of a new year, then announces the Torchlight Parade. From where I'm standing, I see a fiery torch light up at the top of the mountain, followed by another and another and another. Soon, the mountainside looks like it's on fire as skiers weave their way back and forth, holding brilliant flames up to the sky.

My breath catches at the sight. "Beautiful," I say.

D pulls my hair to the side and kisses the back of my ear. "Not near as beautiful as you, Catalina."

Something about hearing him use my full name feels so intimate. So personal. And so filled with love. I turn to face him, and I'm torn between kissing him deeply and exposing my heart to him and shutting down and telling him it's over. But he has plans of his own. He takes my hand and starts pulling me out of the crowd.

"Hey," I say. "What are you doing?"

"I have to tell you something."

DINGANE

I lead us away from the crowd and toward the bright orange hearse that is idling by the ski lodge. Jakeel is right on time. Cat peers up at me through her thick eyelashes with a confused look on her face.

"We have somewhere else to be, kitty cat."

"Oh? *¿Dónde?*"

"It's a surprise," I say and pull her onto my lap once we're inside the warm confines of the car. I wrap my arms around her waist and nod at the Luber driver. He pulls away, turning around to head back toward town and away from the crowd.

When we arrive at the inn, Cat gives me the side eye. "Really? This is the surprise?"

"Patience, babe," I say and help her out of the hearse. Holding hands, we walk side by side to our cabin and upon opening the door, Cat gasps, slowly stepping inside, her eyes wide with wonder.

While we were gone, the cabin was transformed. It's solely illuminated by white candles, and more floral arrangements have been added to the one I gave Cat earlier. Their sweet fragrance fills the small space, which is warm from the fireplace. I had asked the manager, Eva Blackstone, to set everything up while we were gone. My visit to the florists earlier was also to arrange for the flowers to be delivered.

"Did you do all this?" Cat asks.

"Well, I had help. This is why I left earlier."

"Oh."

I guide Cat over to the love seat that faces the fireplace, and she sits down next to me. I turn to face her, continuing to hold her hand.

"Catalina, from the moment we met, I've felt a connection with you beyond anything I've ever experienced. You quiet the storm raging inside of me and fill me with purpose. When I think about where I was even a year ago, I can see how good you are for me, and I hope I am as good for you."

She meets my eyes, but then quickly looks away. I can feel her trying to pull our hands apart, and my heart begins pounding against my chest. This isn't the reaction I anticipated.

"Wait." I squeeze her hand, and she stills. "Please."

I reach for the velvet pouch sitting on top of the coffee table before us and spill the rings out onto the wood surface.

"What are those?" she asks, leaning forward for a closer look. I release her hand so I can grab a ring, and a small gasp escapes her lips.

"I'm not asking you to marry me, don't worry." I can't help but smile when I see her shoulders relax. "Not yet, anyway."

Her head whips up, and her mouth hangs open in shock, which makes me chuckle.

I explain the significance of the juniper and the amazonite, then say, "Consider these promise rings. A promise to be there for each other, whether as lovers or as friends. These rings will be a source of inner peace and healing, something we both still need. Do you accept this gift—this token of friendship and a symbol of our growth together?" I ask her in earnest, hoping she doesn't hear the plea in my tone.

At my words, Cat practically melts, and I imagine the walls crumbling around her. "*Sí, mi Impundulu.* I accept with all my heart."

She flings her arms around my neck and presses her body against mine. We hold each other for a few moments, and when she pulls away, I slip the band on the ring finger, on her right hand, and she does the same to me. The moment the rings are on our fingers, something locks into place. I don't know if it's magic, but it's like our promise to each other is recognized by the universe. A tremor ripples through my body, the scar over my heart twitches, and some of the lingering fear from my past fades away.

Cat places her hand on her heart as her lips part. "Did you feel that?" she asks.

I nod, completely in awe at my connection with her. "I did." Then I add, "We belong together, babe."

She kisses me, then says, "And to think I was going to break up with you tonight."

"Wait, what?"

"You were acting strange, so I thought you were going to break up with me. I was only going to do it to beat you to the punch." Her gaze roams from the ring to the flowers and then to the candles. "Now I understand," she says with a smile.

She straddles me and runs her fingers through my short hair, planting her luscious lips on mine and giving me a deep kiss that is laden with a promise for so much more.

Five years ago, I didn't have a life. Now, I do, and I can choose how I want to live it and who I want to spend it with. And I count my lucky stars to have found someone like Cat. Giving her all of me, we ring in the new year with a promise I hope will last a lifetime.

Meet Cat & D in *Sun & Moon Academy Book One: Fall Semester* and *Sun & Moon Academy Book Two: Spring Semester*

HAPPY HOLIDAYS FROM THE HAVENWOOD FALLS FAMILY!

Stay up to date at www.HavenwoodFalls.com

Subscribe to our reader group and receive free stories and more!